THE UNIVERSE PLAYING STRINGS

The Universe Playing Strings

A NOVEL

R. M. Kinder

University of New Mexico Press ∿ Albuquerque

Library of Congress Cataloging-in-Publication Data
Names: Kinder, R. M. (Rose Marie) author.
Title: The universe playing strings : a novel /
R. M. Kinder.
Description: First edition. | Albuquerque :
University of New Mexico Press, 2016.

Identifiers: LCCN 2015045706 |
ISBN 9780826357410 (softcover : acid-free paper) |
ISBN 9780826357427 (electronic)
Classification: LCC PS3561.I429 U53 2016 (print) |
LCC PS3561.I429 (ebook) | DDC 813/.54—dc23
LC record available at http://lccn.loc.
gov/2015045706

Cover illustration: *Sunday Afternoon,*
©Alice Webb, 2016, oil on canvas
Designed by Lisa Tremaine
Composed in Meridien

To harmony

DRAMATIS PERSONAE

MUSICIANS

Carl Bradshaw
Amy Chandler
Jack Martin
Cora Leban

SET I

Carl

Carl sat on his sofa next to a troubled, lovely woman and decided, as he had done for other women in his life, to make her happy if he could. "What you're saying is you can't get the house without ten thousand dollars?"

She nodded and her black curls bounced just the way that pleased him so, like a little girl's, though she was about thirty-five and, right now, near tears. "Yes, and I've never wanted anything so much in my life as I do that house."

"Well, I think I could help you out," he said.

"You haven't got that kind of money."

He lit a fresh cigarette from the coal of his present one. "Oh, I can usually scrape up whatever I want or need."

"Are you serious? You'd do that? I'd pay you back, Carl."

"Wouldn't be no hurry."

"I can't believe this." She pressed her palms to her cheeks. "Why some woman hasn't snapped you up, I'll never know. You're a godsend."

"Don't bring God into this. I suspect He's not fond of money dealings."

She didn't laugh as he expected she would, but took his hand and kissed the back of it. He was both appalled and touched. "Let's not overdo it now," he said. "It's just money." He stood up. "I need some coffee. How about you?" He went into the kitchen to hide his discomfort, and from there heard more strongly the wind buffeting the house. Some storms came from everywhere all at once, dangerous and unpredictable and fascinating. He fixed coffee and added water to the

3

simmering pot of fruit and spices. He kept the pot on the stove partly for the illusion of cooking and warmth, and largely for the sweet aroma. It made the place seem lived in and welcoming, instead of just being a shelter for a seventy-year-old man whose wife had left him years ago.

He cut a thick slab of store-bought apple pie for himself and a thinner slice for the woman in his living room. He liked her and he didn't like her. She had skin like a white honeysuckle blossom, flawless, soft, the same texture on her arms and hands as on her face. And her eyes were a lustrous, gentle black. Elizabeth. She looked good in anything. He was a sucker for beautiful women, and especially for smart, artistic ones. She was more beautiful than creative, but she moved with real grace, like she should have been a dancer and might have been if given different choices in life.

"You're the sweetest man, Carl," she said. She stood up, put one hand on each side of his face, and kissed him. When she leaned back, he made a light harrumphing sound. "Do that when both my hands ain't full."

"I'm no fool," she said, and laughed.

He knew she wasn't. "You meet me tomorrow for lunch," he said, "and we'll see what we can do about your problem."

꒳

When Carl scooted into the booth, he placed the thick envelope of cash in front of Elizabeth as if it were no more than a napkin. "Here's that bit of help you need," he said.

"Oh." She put her hand on his. "You are the sweetest man I've ever known. I mean that."

"Then it's because you bring it out in me. Besides, you need money right now and right now I got it. Makes sense."

Earlier he had printed a simple note for her to sign, but he was now somehow trapped in the act of giving and couldn't mention the note. Her eyes were too big over the cash, and the place where her collarbones met was so precious he wanted to press his lips right there. Women had fine bones. Fine ways.

"I've never seen so much money in one place," she said.

"Then you've been hanging around with the wrong fellows."

He thought maybe she herself would mention a payback note, but she didn't, so he ate his cobbler and listened to the talk of a happy, planning woman.

"I'm going to put up one of those white fences," she said. "Not the tall ones, the decorative ones." She unfolded a colored advertisement from a local hardware store. "See?"

"That's rolled picket," he said. "Pretty flimsy. Won't hold up."

"No?" She looked dismayed, and something that very moment clued him in that she might be acting. She was too smart a gal not to know something cheap when she saw it. She pushed the ad aside. "Then no fence for me," she said. "Good thing I checked with you."

He lit his after-lunch cigarette, cocked it upward with a set of his jaw, and squinted at her through the smoke. It was a look he had learned from his father, wary but patient, warning onlookers that this person was perhaps more shrewd than he appeared.

"Yep," he said. "Good thing."

Her expression changed slightly, so briefly that it could have been a flicker of reflected shadow from outside, then her flushed happiness returned and she flustered into her purse for lipstick, and her part of the bill, how much was it? Oh, let her pay, please. Then the tip? At least the tip?

"I got all that," he said.

⌁

Later, at his workbench, he felt nagged by his own nature,

uncomfortable with himself. Why had he done that? Been compelled to some dumb, grand gesture? He carefully repaired one tuba, polished it bright yellow gold. He'd been dating Elizabeth for almost eight months, but they hadn't been to bed together yet, due mostly to his own maneuvering. Maybe he'd given her the money because he wasn't going to be able to give her anything else substantial. He turned on the fan behind his desk. What was he worried about? She'd pay him back. Most things turned out pretty well if a person had good intentions. Maybe she was a little conniving and manipulative, but she wouldn't want her name on the county docket. Neither would he.

Finally placing the concern aside, he repaired a trombone, rehaired a fiddle bow, and began removing the frets from a guitar. He was fond of all these instruments, and handled them gently, though his hands were quite thick and stubby. Instruments, like people, should have a healthy glow, should reflect their environment, and these had been, in Carl's opinion, a little mistreated. He refrained from actually speaking to an instrument, though he occasionally muttered "there" or "done" or "how's that?" in its direction.

At four forty-five, with the same slow precision, he cleaned his tools and work area. At five, he donned his hat, coat, gave a friendly nod to his employer and the sales clerks, and sauntered out into the early dark of a winter day. The brisk air stung his cheeks and lungs. He was his own man till Monday morning. He ate supper in town, alone, looking past his image in the windowpane to see the few bundled pedestrians heading for their cars and homes. He liked to think they were all happy people. He was. At six thirty, he drained the remaining coffee from the white mug, put two dollars on the table for the young miss who had served him, winked in her direction, and then drove home to change clothing for his night job. Shortly, dressed in show clothes—dark suit, dark hat, richly carved boots, string tie—he felt younger and fresher. Now he was a fiddler instead of a repairman and he let himself strut a little.

Elizabeth came in during the second set, and the moment was worth all his afternoon's concern. In spite of being one of the biggest and most expensive restaurant-bars in town, it was still a cowboy's place, with pine walls, rough plank tables, metal plates, and simple, hearty food, just steak, beans, and bread. Elizabeth was out of place, and most people turned to watch her pass. Carl, playing fill behind the singer's "Maiden's Prayer," bobbed his head ever so slightly to acknowledge Elizabeth, and was rewarded with her miming a quick kiss to him. When the band took a breather, Carl joined her at the musicians' table. She was all gratitude, though of course she never mentioned money where the others could hear. Neither did Carl. She squeezed his hand under the table, leaned in to kiss his cheek twice, and whispered quick plans and happy thoughts: "I can close on Monday, maybe, and move in during the week." "I never believed I could own a house of my own." "I'm so excited I can barely sit still." "I should be packing." "You are the dearest friend."

During the third set, she discreetly waved a couple of times, and he realized she wanted to leave. He understood. When a woman got a possible happiness in her head, she immediately had to rush pell-mell toward it, for fear it'd get away from her. Elizabeth would be packing and purchasing for the next few days. Weeks, maybe. Months.

On Saturday night, Carl again expected Elizabeth to come, though her custom was to come on either Friday or Saturday, not both. As the evening wore on, he got more and more irritated with the diners, with their clanking silverware, their shrill laughs and whoops. Usually he was patient, understanding that most people, especially men, wanted a few drinks before getting on the dance floor. But he didn't feel like catering to anyone at the moment. He played only for his fiddle and himself, to see how much richness he could pull out of the thin, delicate wood. Fiddles could cry if the player had the right touch.

Elizabeth never came. When a die-hard couple asked for one more swing tune, Carl mumbled to Leroy, "Let's call it quits." He played a waltz instead, a slow one, and avoided looking at the dancers' faces. The couple waltz-stumbled up to the mic.

"Pick it up," the man said. "Need some goddamn life. We asked for swing."

Carl nodded, as if a swing was exactly what they'd play next, though he had no intention of providing more show-off time for a churlish drunk. People were merry as long as the music was what they wanted. If not, they could turn mean. During the steel-guitar break, Carl lit a cigarette and let it dangle from his lips while the band finished out the waltz. This was a sad, dying song and the set was over whether the dancing couple liked it or not.

♪

"You're worrying over nothing," he said to his grizzled reflection Sunday morning. He slapped shaving cream onto his cheeks and chin. "If you're going to worry about money, then keep it so you know where it's at." He hung around the house all day, puttering things into neatness, waiting for the phone to ring. He was determined not to call Elizabeth and not to drive by her place. "Give the woman time," he reminded himself. "Women got their own idea of time." Midafternoon, he sat at the kitchen table, sipping coffee and looking out onto gray, windswept fields. So many songs always mixed rain and sadness, cold weather and grief. That was no accident and no lie.

He had a gut-wrenched feeling.

♪

Midweek, Webb Tucker sauntered up to Carl's repair counter and laid an octagonal bow down gently. "Hate to let go of this even for a day," Webb said, "but it needs rehairing and I'm just not too good at that." He had large eyes, a deep blue that left an immediate favorable impression, which closer acquaintance had dispelled. Carl lifted the bow.

"Don't see many of this make anymore."

"Could you do it today?"

"I'm pretty booked up."

"I just learned about a contest over in Wheatwater Friday and Saturday. I'd like to have my best bow. You going?"

"Wheatwater? Hadn't heard about it."

"There's no senior category. You'd have to play against the young bucks."

"That wouldn't bother me any more than it does you. But I didn't ask off work. I've about had it with contests anyway."

"I can understand that."

Carl didn't glance up, but he knew the expression he'd see if he did. "Probably not the way I do," he said. He stood, picked up a red tag. "If there's no repair needed, I can have it for you by ten tomorrow morning. That good enough?"

"Great."

Carl tied the tag to the bow. He rehaired it on his own time. He had the proper equipment, and he completed the process patiently, finally applying rosin gradually, and using one of his own fiddles to test the smoothness of the play. He wondered if Tucker was the kind of man to blame losing on someone who had touched his bow in the last couple days.

⌣

When Tucker came for the bow, he held it up to the light, lowered it, tightened the hair. "Flat as a ribbon. You did a fine job."

"Of course. It's a fine bow."

9

"How much do I owe you? Do I pay you or the cashier?"

"You don't owe anything. I did it at home."

"I don't want free work."

"Well, you got it."

"Tell you what. If I win that contest, I'll tell them you fixed my bow. How's that? I'll be your best advertising."

"I'd rather you didn't."

Tucker took a small knife from his pocket, opened it. He lifted the bow with his other hand. "Looks like we can't come to an agreement."

"Looks like." Carl struck a match to his cigarette. He assumed Tucker was going to cut the strands and then he'd have to make the next move, and Tucker the next, and so on. "Guess you could cut off my work," he said, "and render the bow useless a few days. Seems a pity, since it's not my workmanship we're quarreling about."

"You're not giving me any choice. I'm not going to be one of your charity cases."

"Thirty dollars," Carl grunted. "You made your point."

Tucker placed some bills on the counter. "A good fiddle deserves a good bow, don't you think?" His lips were twisted in a sideways grin. "I mean the sweeter the instrument, the straighter that bow's got to be. Right?" He held Carl's eyes for a moment, then strode away. He had a real manly walk, straight-backed, long-legged, smooth. He wore his jeans too tight, though, for a workingman. Carl dry-spit to his left. But then Tucker wasn't advertising himself as a workingman. This had to do with Elizabeth.

Carl tried to settle his mind on the tasks at hand. Then he gave up. He slipped into his coat, told his boss he'd be back in an hour or so, and fired his truck toward Elizabeth's. Two trucks were outside her house, both half-filled with furniture. He pulled on by, circled around, and parked half a block away, facing her driveway. "Someone's got to help her," he muttered. "You think you could load up a whole house for her?"

Soon, three men exited the house, two carrying a thick mattress and one, Webb Tucker, carrying box springs. Behind came Elizabeth, struggling with bed slats. She was a small thing. Even now, he had the urge to get out, stride up, and take those burdensome slats from her. But Webb was doing that this very moment, and apparently saying something personal at the same time—Carl recognized the way Elizabeth ducked her head, like an embarrassed child. Lord, she *was* a striking woman. Untamed, black mane of hair. She was wearing a yellow shirt and slacks, and Carl had never seen her in yellow. She was like a damned orchid, so beautiful she made his throat hurt.

He endured the discomfort of watching till the trucks pulled away, each full. Elizabeth stood in the yard alone, looking after them, then walked back to the house. At the door she turned and gazed directly down the street where Carl had parked. He didn't believe she could recognize his vehicle from where she stood, especially just by a head-on view, but he felt as if she had.

"I should just parade naked and get it over with." Instead of driving forward, he backed up an entire block and around an intersection corner, where he could drive as he normally did, prudently and legally.

He returned to the music store, forced his attention where it belonged till his shift was over. Then he ate dinner stoically, as if he were fueling an old machine. At home, after arguing with himself about pride, genuine pride, false pride, falls, and fools, he dialed her number.

An operator directed him to the new one. He waited for calm to come before he dialed again.

"Who is this?" she answered.

"You know who this is."

"Carl? Oh. Damn. I kept planning to call you, and time just got away."

He did want to believe her. He wished he could see her face. "Don't stay away, gal. I miss you."

11

"Of course you do," she said in a throaty whisper. "Don't worry. I'll be back."

Then she dropped her playful voice and became Elizabeth the busy homemaker who still had so much unpacking to do, had no moments to spare, but would soon. When they hung up, he felt worse. He smoked three cigarettes at his kitchen table and listened to the Oklahoma wind. So he knew. Okay. He made a new pot of coffee just for the soothing rhythm of the percolator.

Surely God had made a few good women.

↵

Carl sold his house and land in the spring, not because he had to. He wasn't broke. Even before the sale, he had more than twice what he'd given Elizabeth. Overall, he moved simply because he didn't want to live out his remaining days where he'd been a fool too many times. He could, he supposed, have sued Elizabeth for the ten thousand. And he might have won—surely his word carried a great deal of weight in town. But he had no proof; he'd have to ask around about witnesses, maybe approach her personally. She hadn't once called, once come by. Her debt would be hard to prove, and besides, he'd actually been hung by his own ego and stupidity. Justice had been meted. The whole county didn't need to know about it. By leaving, he would be saying that ten thousand wasn't worth anything to him. A trifling sum for a trifling woman.

He bought a better used car, rented a U-Haul, and gave away everything but his tools, clothes, and music paraphernalia. He worried most about his record collection and put those boxes in the car where he could control the temperature. The albums were part of his history, even his might-have-been. He had been the first fiddler with the group Prairie Sons. But he had backed out when they got a real manager and were going on the road. He had been afraid to leave his wife and afraid to take her along. He had called Billy Wilcox, a young fiddler, and told him to be hanging around the Veterans Hall the next morning. "I'll break the news to the guys and hand you over to them. They'll be pleased at the swap, I guarantee. Have your fiddle. Have your things packed and be ready to travel." Billy left with the band. And the band made it big. Now, every time Carl heard one of their songs on the radio, he felt a slight curl of pain at the fiddle breaks. Billy had learned some of those from him. When Billy came through Oklahoma, he'd look up Carl and run through some tunes. They'd eat together. Carl liked Billy. He was glad to have sent him on. Now Carl thought maybe it wasn't loss he felt, but something petty like jealousy, and he didn't want to own up to it. Billy's name was all over the states, in music history.

And where was Carl? Driving west away from a woman, foolhardiness, memories, and misery. Seventy, with nothing but music and a bitter taste if he let it rise. He didn't. He studied the change in scenery, flipped through the music stations. He couldn't get anything clear, but he recalled an Indian banjo player who had come from Arizona. That was the direction he was headed.

⌣

Carl liked coming into Tucson, the long sweep down into a valley, with wide blue sky above it, a sharp white sun, giant saguaros reaching up arms that had taken a hundred years or more to grow. Looked like a place for old age, peace, and space.

On the third day, after reconnoitering the layout of the town, he rented a four-room run-down box house, one of twelve grouped together and scattered around at different angles. The arrangement created the illusion, Carl supposed, of a separate yard for each house, and made the grouping seem like a real neighborhood, maybe a village. That was okay by him. He didn't mind being a loner, but being lonely was another matter. He read want ads and strolled around downtown, hitting music stores. Stone's Emporium was looking for a repairman to replace a guy who had just quit with no notice. Dave Stone squired him past racks and racks of instruments to a workshop in the back—a counter facing the store side, a swinging gate allowing access, and the three inner walls lined with shelves. Grease and dust stained the worktable, bench, and floor. Small boxes, waxy with grime, held a jumble of instrument parts. "Guess you're not a musician," Carl said.

"What makes you say that?"

"Just looking around."

Stone bristled. "The help does the cleaning. The repairman keeps his shop like he wants it."

"That'll take some doing, but I guess I could make it mine."

He'd work there five days a week from nine to five, and Saturdays from nine to twelve. No vacation time, no benefits. Any days off docked his pay.

"I'm working for the discipline more than the money," he said, "or I'd turn you down. A man has to keep busy."

He took off his jacket and began cleaning. In less than thirty minutes Dave Stone appeared again.

"The cleaning can wait. We have a backlog of repairs."

"I don't work in a sty." Carl stretched up as tall as he could and reared back, smoke floating up from the cigarette between his lips. "Want me to leave? Happy to do it."

Stone quickly considered that option. "Just don't spend the whole damn day cleaning."

Carl continued separating tools and parts from debris. He ignored the silent presence of the other man. When Stone walked away, Carl found the bathroom, sudsed up some water in a bucket, and carried it to his station. He cleaned till noon, hauled boxes of trash out the back, washed himself up as best he could, then headed toward the front door. "I threw a bunch of junk away," he called to Stone. "Don't drag it in while I'm gone." He strolled down to the restaurant he had decided would be his daily rest. They served solid food, without any fancy names to raise the price. Pork steaks, mashed potatoes, corn bread, stewed tomatoes, and applesauce. Real food. He'd have to establish the kind of service he liked— friendly and prompt. He'd tip well. At exactly 1:00 p.m. he went back through the Emporium doors, sat down at the wooden table at his now somewhat-orderly workstation, lit a cigarette, and began dismantling an alto sax. When it was repaired, he riffed through a bit of "Sweet Georgia Brown" and two people in the store stopped to listen.

Then, his practical side firmly positioned, he went looking for a band that needed a fiddler for a regular gig at a steak house or something similar, two nights a week, danceable music.

Amy

Amy Chandler sat on the floor of Stone's Emporium beneath the long rack of Martin guitars. She was fair skinned and black haired, slender, but with a generous bosom that she sometimes hated because it hampered her guitar picking. She was dressed as usual, in a loose white blouse and a long, gathered print skirt, clothing that allowed her body both disguise and freedom. Now she held the Martin D-28 across her knees and played. She had to have the Martin. She had to. The bass notes rang, popped. She bobbed a little as the fingers of her left hand danced from chord to chord. She burst into song. "Cause I got leaving in the soles of my feet," *chunk, chunk, chunk*, run the bass up, up, up, hammer oooonnnnn. "Not staying in the key to the door, I'm telling you baby that I'm gonna leave," walk to the next chord, delay, hammer blues high, "since you don't want me anymore."

Oh. She wanted this guitar. She ran her right palm over the side and bottom, lifted the guitar and sighted down the strings. A short, bowlegged guy dressed in a brown suit and wearing a tall brown hat stood at the end of the row.

"Pretty fine picking," he said.

"I was mostly singing."

"Heard that too. Feel like a little company?"

She didn't answer and he turned away. She thought he had gone and she went back to worrying about the asking price for the Martin. Fourteen hundred fifty. She had nine hundred in savings and a paycheck due Friday. Rent due Friday. Groceries. Gas money.

The old gent was back with a fiddle in his hand. He was tuning it quickly. That meant he could play.

"'Ragtime Annie'?" he said, and just went into the tune. She slipped the Martin into position. They played six songs in a row. He'd switch and she'd follow. When he stopped, she slapped her knee and cackled.

"We got to play together some more," she said.

She followed him to the repair counter, chattering about wanting the guitar, about being late for work, about a place called The Kettle where people jammed on Friday nights.

"You're sort of a whole crowd by yourself, aren't you?" he said.

"I'm talking too much?"

"Couldn't happen. Not around me."

"You got to jam with us," she said. "This town's only got one fiddler who comes close to you. Paul Welford. And he doesn't come that close."

"Don't make more of me than I am. How late does the place stay open?"

"Depends. If there's a good crowd, could go till two a.m."

"I got a gig on the weekends out at Sam's Steak Place."

"You're kidding! I thought Mel's Flying Texans played there."

"Do. Just joined them."

"Damn." She clenched a hand as if she'd snap that opportunity out of the air. "You and me could've started a band. We still could, you know. How about it?"

"Nope. I don't spread myself that thin, and I already shook hands on the first deal."

She got his name, phone number, and address and jotted her own down on a scrap of paper. Then she flipped it over and sketched a quick map. "This is to The Kettle, coming from Sam's. The doors open around seven. Open mic starts at eight. People come and go, though most of them stay. You've got to come by."

"I'll do that very thing. I'd like to hear you and your friends." Carl stuck the note in his shirt pocket.

"Nice to meet you, Mr. Bradshaw," she said.

"You could drop the mister or call me Pop."

Twice that afternoon he read the note again. She had a firm writing style, half-cursive, half-print, real legible and feminine. The map was bold strokes. Feisty little thing. He remembered her bright eyes. She was a fireball but friendly. And she was no fool with that guitar, either. She didn't just *talk* about playing, she played.

On Friday's lunch hour, Amy drove to the Emporium and went past the cluttered front counter and Dave Stone right to the workshop. Her newfound fiddler was removing pegs from a mandolin. His thick, broad hands were surprisingly deft.

"Now you're a pretty sight to look up and see," he said.

"I'm going to buy that Martin," she said. "I can't get it out of my mind. You pull any weight around here?"

"Just what's on my bones. Don't want any more."

"What do you think the Martin's worth?"

"Nine fifty with no case. If you tell them I said so, though, I could lose my job. I'd like to keep it awhile."

She headed back toward the front. Carl left his station and walked up the aisle. The afternoon sun shone dust haze all across the front of the store, like it drew dirt up from the floor. He stood where he could watch the transaction without being seen. Amy was coming back through the front door, carrying a battered black guitar case held together with silver tape. She opened it on the floor, pulled out a Guild, and glanced up at Stone. "What'll you give me for this?"

"Maybe one fifty."

"You haven't even looked at it."

"Can see it from here."

"What's it worth as a trade-in?"

"Guess we could go two hundred."

She chewed at the nail of her right index finger for a minute. "How about you take the Guild, I keep my old case and pay you seven hundred for the Martin?"

Stone considered the far wall of drums, the sound equipment. He was a tall, lean, brown man, with a downturned mouth and half-moon sags under his eyes.

"Not today," he said.

She threw up her hands and shut her guitar case. "Did my best." She squatted to lock it and her red-flowered skirt spread out on the dirty floor. Her hands were quick. She stood, gripped the handle, and started toward the door.

"Nine hundred." Stone said.

"Eight."

"Okay. Okay." Dave Stone had the receipt pad in front of him.

Carl went back to his station and hummed while he worked. He was glad the girl had had enough sense not to come back there like they'd been in cahoots.

She called him a few minutes later.

"You have to come by The Kettle tonight, okay? I've told a bunch of people about you."

"You have a job or you just run around digging up musicians?"

"I'm a cartographer at County Planning. I'm pretty good at what I do."

"Bet you are," he said, and tried to sound a little suggestive. Later he thought he probably sounded like a horny old dude and he was both embarrassed and proud. Elizabeth crept into his mind and he booted her out by thinking of Amy's warm voice and her assertion, "I'm pretty good at what I do." Women could spice up life, that was certain.

Amy called County Planning too. "I'm really sick," she lied.

"I guess it's what I had for lunch. I'm reeling." At home, she removed the old strings from the Martin and polished the wood till it shone circles of deep brown. She put on new strings. Then she played and got lost. Time turned slow and precious. She was in love with this room and the ringing sound. She wanted the world to hear this music. After four, she began phoning friends to see who was going to The Kettle. "I got a new guitar," she said to each one and waited for the delicious question, "What'd you get?"

"A D-28. Same age as me and twice as mellow."

When it was near time for George to come home, she became aware of her situation. The ironing board she had used that morning still stood in front of the window. The scrambled-eggs skillet and plate were in the sink. And there was the Martin—evidence of her indulgence, her wayward-ness. She put the guitar in her old case and leaned it in its corner spot. "Sorry, baby." Now she had to work.

All the fun of the day had gone, drained like bubble bath out of the tub. She chewed a fingernail, plodded into the kitchen, and ran hot water into the sink, added soap. She was suddenly tired. Why did it matter if George didn't like dirty dishes? It was *her* place. His moods wore her down. Much of the time he looked like Simon Legree or at least like a cartoon sketch she had once seen of Legree, all narrow lines and dark glower. George even twisted his moustache and avoided meeting people's eyes. He made nasty little jabs at her all the time.

But he was the best she'd found. Not the best musician, just the best music and bed partner. He was sort of ugly during lovemaking, all gusto and lip smacking, but she actually found that exciting. Here she was, a little too skinny in the lower half and maybe too pushy with a man who enjoyed her company, who made love to her like she was his favorite food, and yet she was dreading his coming home. She wanted too much. A lot of women would be grateful to have some-one like George. She went into the bedroom to rest for just a minute. The bed whooshed pleasantly and fully beneath her. She liked sleeping too. She wasn't lazy, but she got bored easily. So many good things in life.

She woke to George sitting down heavily on the bed. "You cut work again?"

He could always tell. She didn't know how. "I got *so* sick," she muttered. "I vomited three or four times."

"Skipping The Kettle, too?"

"That's hours away. Maybe I'll feel better."

"Sure you will. You always feel better for what you want to do." He whistled down the hall. A few minutes later she padded into the living room. She heard him scooting things around in the kitchen. He came in with a sandwich for himself. He never, ever, fixed food for her. Never even asked. Now he sat on the sofa, leafing through a *Frets* magazine, and taking very small, irritating bites of the sandwich.

"Maybe I should try to eat something," she said.

"Maybe."

She was supposed to be sick, so she stayed where she was. When he finished, he brushed his hands, opened the Hershey's tin on the coffee table, and rolled a joint from the stash.

"If you don't go," he said, "I'm going to do a set alone. 'Rock Salt and Nails,' 'Weave and Way,' and 'Jerusalem Ridge.'"

"Good set. What if I go, too, but we perform separately? We'd surprise everybody."

"No. When we go there together, we're a duet."

They'd been through this before. She knew his real reason. If she went onstage alone, people would know she was pretty good without George Dey. He wasn't too hot by himself. Sort of a vapid musician, all thin arty looks, difficult riffs but like a string of perfect pearls, every note just like the others. She was a little ashamed of herself for thinking that way.

She went in the kitchen and was slicing cheese when she

heard a case opening. She hurried to the doorway of the living room. Sometimes he played her guitar. He was opening her case. "What's this?" He lifted out the Martin, looked at her with those black marble eyes. Now she really did feel ill. "Got a good deal on it," she said. "Couldn't pass it up."

"How good?" He ran scales perfectly, full circle. "Nice sound. Good action. How good a deal?"

"The Guild and five hundred."

"I don't believe you." He laid the guitar down carefully and stood. He glanced around the room, located her purse, and went to it.

"What's it matter?" she said. "George. We're not even married. It's my money."

He had dumped her purse on the floor. He opened her checkbook, looked at the last stub. "Lying bitch," he said. "I'm out of here." He put the Martin in the case, latched it. "George," she said. "Don't take it." He ignored her, walked outside, left the door open. He set the case in the backseat of the car, easily. He drove away without once looking back. She stayed at the front door for a while, feeling anguish, but not about George. She didn't want him to break in the guitar. That was for her to do.

She thought about going to The Kettle herself. It might cause trouble. George had never actually beat her up, and she wouldn't have stayed with him if he had, but he'd shaken her hard a number of times, and poked his sharp fingers into the soft flesh under her collarbones. That gave her nickel-sized bruises that he said were "nothing." He got worse bruises, he said, from their lovemaking. What she dreaded most, though, was the black silent anger he could sustain for days, no matter how she coaxed. He punished her offenses with silence, and oh, was silence hard on her. She liked peace and harmony. Didn't she? Did she provoke problems? She should stay home now. George would feel vindicated, like he got even with her. It was settled. She would stay home. It would be god-awful difficult to do, but she would do it.

She cleaned the living room and kitchen, moving slowly, without the natural grace she had when she was happy. This was hateful work. She couldn't handle doing the bedroom too—clothes everywhere, magazines, empty glasses. She undressed and lay naked on the bed.

❧

Amy slept, woke to George nudging her. He smelled like beer, and alcohol wasn't served at The Kettle. He stroked her sloppily and slid on top of her like she was just a sheet. He couldn't come. "Baby, baby, baby," he said. "I don't know what I'm going to do with you. You won't learn." He was too drunk to keep his anger awake. When he fell asleep, she washed herself, put on panties and a T-shirt, and sat on the living room floor to play her new Martin. The stereo clock said 4:00 a.m. The Kettle never ran that long. George had gone somewhere else. She sang a few old ballads and thought how sad they were and how the Martin just almost cried. That guitar was as sweet as a baby.

Saturday morning, she got a call from Carl.

"That was a good map you drew," he said. "Led me right to The Kettle and a horde of musicians. One of them had your new guitar. Now," she heard him draw on a cigarette, then his husky voice resumed, "you need any help getting it back?"

"You went!" she said. "Damn, and I missed it!" She took the phone into the kitchen. There, holding the receiver in position with her shoulder, happy and hungry, she scooped tiny teaspoons of ice cream from a half-gallon container and talked with Carl about people he had met at The Kettle. Gary Hargrove, uh-huh, a regular, a good old guy too. Amy liked him fine. Bob Burden, giant banjo player. Ummmm.

Fair musician, but wanted to be treated like the best. Milosh Lukovich. Sort of sappy, but a nice guy. "Eats, sleeps, and breathes music," she said. Welford wasn't there? Not a surprise. When he did come, he was competing more than jamming. "He comes early and leaves early," she said. "You caught just a few of the late crew."

And finally, "Yeah. That was my guitar." She waved the spoon, feeling guilty about discussing George while he slept. She kept her voice low, aware of George sleeping in the bedroom and how he could come down a hall so silently and be right behind her. She turned now, to peek around the doorframe. "I wasn't feeling well and he wanted to play it. I broke it in though." She recalled that she actually had. "I played it all afternoon before he got home." She asked who George had jammed with, if he had left alone.

"A couple young guys were trying to play with him. Banjo and guitar. They couldn't keep up. I don't know when he left."

After she hung up and returned the ice cream to the freezer, she opened the living room drapes. Even if George had been playing with some cute girls, she wouldn't have been jealous. Maybe she was hoping he *had* been with someone. She snuggled down on the sofa, the sun lapping over her and lulling her toward sleep. Tomorrow afternoon she was going to jam with her new fiddler. Carl Bradshaw. Pop Bradshaw. Music. Sleep.

Jack

When his father left for DC, Jack Martin took full control of the white ranch house. He walked around naked when he wanted to. He drank beer and lined the empty bottles up on the long wooden table in the dining room. He smoked and filled the ashtrays with butts. His father had had bookcases built on almost every wall of the house, and Jack tried counting the books he'd read. He quit when he realized the number was going to be minuscule and his father had probably read every damned one of them. "Every damned one," he said aloud a few times, in the empty house with no curtains on the windows. He kept his guitar out and played it for hours in front of the fireplace. He fried a steak and heated some beans. Good solid food for the son of a famous, no-nonsense man. He lay on his bed to masturbate and then couldn't because it seemed like a kid thing to do on a Texas November day. He had nothing to do but wait, wait for a problem to arise or a cousin to call, or to need or want something.

"What have you got planned, Jack?" his father had asked. "You want to go to Virginia?"

"Nope. Don't know."

"You could maybe get into a school at semester break. Just if you wanted."

"Nope."

"You want to come to DC with me?"

"Nope."

"Well, in a week or so, I'll be flying to California. If you want to join me, give me a call and I'll arrange the flight."

27

"Okay."

He prided himself on these short, to-the-point responses. He didn't plan on going to California.

His cousin Billy drove out the day before Thanksgiving. He had a beer before the fire, smoked three of Jack's cigarettes, and said he had "got laid." It was at a fraternity party, Billy said, and it was his opinion that everyone there got laid that night.

"They left two by two, every which way," he said.

"Like the ark," Jack said.

"Fucking ark."

They both laughed, but Jack stared at the popping coals and felt cheated. He was a no-man in a man's country. He had a father whose books were becoming movies—Jack had had a minor part in one when he was eleven; he played a nine-year-old brat and did it well—and now he had a cousin who had a way with women, something Jack suspected he himself didn't have and never would. He liked them very much, as did his father; he thought of them most of the time. He liked the turn of their ankles and wrists, the secret of them, the scent he couldn't identify but knew the moment it was present, the sweet oil of a lovely young woman.

So he left the evening after Billy announced his coup. He thought of it as "lighting out." He rushed through the ranch house in the sunset hour, when loneliness seemed most natural to him, like the earth was going to sigh itself to death, and he packed all his albums in the metal crates he had used during his one year in college, and grabbed the clothes most dear to him, those different from his father's and uncles' and even his friends'—jeans too short, with knees bursting through, flannel shirts washed and dried so often they wouldn't stay buttoned over his skinny chest. He packed his guitar and the wooden trunk his mother had given him when he was two. It was filled with bits of junk and bits of treasure: a favored fishing reel, guitar strings, harmonicas

28

without their cases, check stubs, deposit slips, notes from his father, matchbooks, spiral notebooks with scratched lyrics he knew by heart now.

He hummed across the Texas night, the white moon scudding cold and low on the horizon, and he got afraid of wrecking somewhere in the dark and no one knowing he had died, so he started a song about that and reworked the lyrics and melody all the way to New Mexico and daytime sleep in a sleazy motel. He tried to call his father from there, but no one answered the DC phone or the California phone, and Josie, his father's Tucson lady, said she thought Lester was in New York.

Jack sat naked on the motel sheets, his bony shanks covered with gooseflesh, and thought he'd be damned if he was kid enough to call his mother or grandmothers. If he died here, he died. He put his guitar on the side of the bed and fell asleep with the palm of his right hand against the guitar's bottom curve.

When he reached Tucson, he called Josie just to say, "I'm in town." She pressed him to come for dinner, and maybe even stay at her place. He refused. "Think I'll check out the music scene," he said. "If Lester calls, tell him I've changed hunting grounds."

He thought that was a stupid thing to have said, not worthy of him at all, absolutely cliché stock character, and he cringed each time he thought of it.

The first music outlet he found was The Mill, where college kids sat on the nighttime glassed-in patio, drinking beer from Mason jars. When Jack had a set on the porch stage, they mostly ignored him. He would sing "Maybelline" or "Evangeline" or "Rag Momma Rag" and sometimes a bright-eyed girl would look his way or some young man with close-cropped hair would clap loudly and drunkenly. Sometimes a voice would call out, "Know any Gordon Lightfoot?" "Know any Hot Tuna?" "Know any . . . ?" but mostly he played to deaf ears and to his absent father and future while he watched the meandering healthy, normal college students lighten the dark streets with color, young lives blurring this corner, that corner, this building, those stairs.

⌣

A young girl left her table of friends and stood right in front of the stage looking up at Jack. She wore a white blouse with lace across the bodice. Her hair was long and deep brown, haloed by the patio lights.

"I'd like to sing 'Willing,'" she said.

"Come on up."

He didn't care if she could sing or not. But she could. When she finished and the crowd applauded—her table the most—he felt as if he had slept with her; no matter who she sat beside or who she went home with, he had somehow beat them all. When his set was over, and he was putting his guitar in the case, he kept glancing her way, hoping she'd read his thoughts and come over. She didn't. So he stopped by her, braced the wooden table with one hand, and bent down to whisper, "What's your name?"

"Marie," she said.

"Can I call you?" He could feel the fraternity chill and his own Ichabod Crane stiffness, but he stayed leaning.

"Why don't you come to The Kettle Friday night?" she said, and he nodded okay and walked away awkwardly, though he tried to move easily, as his father did, with successful grace, with the smoothness of intelligence and talent recognized and rewarded. He knew, though, that his own walk was jagged, shoulder to the left, to the right, to the left. He couldn't move straight even if someone walled him into a maze.

He thought of her every day that week and every night.

"I met this girl," he told his father over the phone. "She joined me for a set. Good singer."

"Are you thinking about enrolling at the university?"

"Nope."

"Whatever you want. The movie deal's gone through on *Lost Country*. If you'd like a part, I'll see what I can do."

"A music part?"

"I don't know. We'd have to write it in."

"Don't do anything special for me." He didn't mean that, but he wanted to mean it.

On Friday, he looked up "Kettle" in the phone book and panicked when it wasn't there. He threw the phone book to the floor and then showered. Maybe she'd made it up. Maybe her name wasn't even Marie and everyone at her table had been laughing at his gullibility. He put on a David Bromberg T-shirt and a blue flannel button-up. He forgot to comb his hair before it dried, and it began to fall in wiry finger curls except where pressed flat and straight under his Budweiser cap.

The musicians hanging around The Mill had heard about The Kettle and a couple had played there. "It's not for you," a young guy said. "Believe me. You got to play country to fit in there."

They quarreled among themselves in a friendly way, but Jack learned what he needed to. The Kettle was not a place; it was a happening at a place. Some do-good organization allowed community use of their ground-floor, street-side rooms. During the week, the building housed religious youth meetings, yoga classes, self-help lectures, and even exercise classes. But on Friday nights, in the two huge rooms, music. Open stage. Folk. Blues. Fiddle. No rock, no sir, no way. "They sort of crowd us out, you know? Lots of old folks in the audience."

"They won't know what to do with Jack." They made some crude suggestions, all in fun.

"I told a girl I'd meet her," Jack said, glad that it was true.

Marie was as beautiful as he had remembered, and single-minded—she wanted to perform. He couldn't fault her for that.

"Would you mind backing me up?" she said. "I don't know the chords to 'Willing.' And how about 'Love Hurts'? You know that one?"

They practiced on the back walk of The Kettle, cars pulling into and out of the Laundromat some yards away. Jack felt sorry for every dude who did his washing on Friday night. He played the best guitar he could. He would play all night to keep her there.

Onstage, he felt they were a couple and that everyone in the audience would assume so. Her love songs were to him. He was glad he had long hair and steel-rimmed glasses, glad he looked like Arlo Guthrie. His Red Wing shoes tapped rhythm for her, his guitar rolled rich behind her voice.

When Marie finally invited him to her apartment, it was to practice her songs. The desert winter stayed bland, played summer. Marie served him tea in frosted glasses, emptied his ashtray, wore pink shorts, white shorts, the cuffs ironed flat, the round brown rim of her buttocks sometimes visible.

He had yet to kiss her.

One afternoon Marie started crying for no good reason. He had never comforted a woman before, but now he understood why his father never let a female friend go. He wanted to be available always, so she wouldn't cry again.

"Whatever it is," he said, "I'll help." He stroked her hair and wondered that he knew how to do that.

He ended up driving her all the way to Colorado the next weekend. She sat in the front seat of his pickup, her suitcases, boxes, and guitar in the back. Her long dark hair was down and when the windows of the pickup were open, the hair teased all around his right side and he cursed himself while he clenched his cigarette between his teeth.

"I'll never forget this," she said.

"I'll marry you if you want. I mean it."

"Maybe. I got to think about it. I don't know."

She stared out the window and he wanted to ask who she was thinking about, which one it was. He thought she'd volunteer the name, but she didn't.

"You're the nicest guy in the world," she said after a while. "Not many men would do this, just drop everything to help somebody."

"You're not just anybody."

He realized that maybe he was, to her, but still he charged all the gas on the card his father had given him when he bought him the truck. He paid for the meals, drove straight through to avoid having to deal with getting a room.

They arrived in her town at one in the morning. Snow drifts scalloped her yard. He scuffled a boot path for her and held her elbow till she was on the porch, carried her things up while she waited for her mother to waken and open the door.

The mother didn't seem to want to invite him in, so Marie walked him to his truck. She leaned against him and he sort of patted her back. She pulled his head down and kissed him long and hard. Her nose and lips were cold but he would have stayed pressed together without moving till the sun rose except that her mother called "Marie" from the doorway.

"Thank you, Jack," she whispered.

He got in the truck and tapped out another cigarette, waiting till she was in the house. Then he gunned the engine and sped down the neat little Colorado street, up some others, headlights spinning into snow, and onto the freeway. When the sun came up, he was still a virgin and on his way to Tucson again. This, at least, his father had never written about, helping a pregnant girl get back home. He wrote a song about it while he drove. When the sun went down, he again got afraid of being on the road without someone

33

knowing where he was. He checked into a motel in the next small town, sprawled across the bed, and watched a music video channel till it signed off the air. He raised a Coke can to the channel's logo, a long-shot picture of Earth.

"You're mine," he said.

⌣

Jack signed up for two courses, astronomy and beginning piano. The piano class was at 8:00 a.m., an outrageous hour since no true musician would get up before noon, but he wanted to be advancing toward a career in some way. Sometimes he trudged up to campus just to practice and couldn't find one open keyboard.

"Buy a piano," his father said.

"Waste of money."

"Not if you want it. You can always sell it later if you want to move on."

"I'm thinking about moving on anyway," he said. That was always a safe desire, because his father couldn't stay still for long either and believed restlessness and unhappiness to be part of budding manhood. It irked Jack that he couldn't experience many things his father hadn't written about, and then he was irked because even *that* feeling was supposed to be standard in the developing buck. The trouble with being raised by smart people is that their wisdom made you second-guess yourself all the time and that stopped you like a two-by-four to the face.

"I'll probably stick it out," Jack said. "I don't want to waste the tuition."

"I don't mind. We're going to do really well from *Lost Country* and they're already asking about my next book. I've almost finished a screenplay on an old murder in South Carolina. I think it'll sell."

It amazed him that his father had a mental life engaged in

other eras, places where he could be villain or hero, where he rode with cowboys, fought with Indians, and was a young man growing up over and over again.

"I've written some more songs," Jack said. "Haven't been totally derelict."

"Make a tape of them. I'll do something for you."

"Maybe."

"I've been thinking about giving you a machine shop for your birthday. It used to be a blacksmith shop, which I assume will please you. I bought it last year and it's doing well. You could have the profits instead of a check from me."

"That might feel good."

"I'll arrange it when I get time. You know I didn't mean you had to live on that money only."

Yeah. He knew.

Jack dropped his classes the next week. He was, after all, the son of a famous man, and he didn't have to do things the way of the mundane world. Maybe he was going to turn into something anytime now.

He slept till noon each day, practiced the harmonica after his shower, walked down to The Mill and had a hoagie. Sometimes he did a set. He drank each evening. He knew every young man's manhood came along with liquor.

He was contemptuous of The Kettle crew, but grudgingly and gradually warmed to some of them, tagging along with Michael Halloran and Milosh Lukovich when they did serious drinking. Jack could hold his own with anyone but the big Serbian. One night Milosh put out shot glasses and two bottles of Slivovitz, plum brandy. Jack stopped just short of vomiting. Halloran fell asleep on the worn green rug. Through a nauseating haze, Jack watched Milosh have five more shots, roll a joint, take two deep drags, then try to wake Halloran. "Come on," he insisted, still firm voiced. "Let's play some hoop, man, the night is young."

Jack liked the red-haired woman Cora okay, though he

wasn't sure if he should approve of her, much less like her. She had a nice voice, but she was pretty old to be hanging out at such a place on Friday nights. She had two kids in college. She reminded him somewhat of his mother, though Cora was probably not as intelligent and maybe not as gutsy. Jack was two when his mother moved out. Afterward, he knew her as this charming, beautiful woman who brought him expensive, tasteful gifts and seemed deeply fond of him. She was a cool blonde and taught Milton at a college back east. She spent summers in Europe, researching. He assumed she always had lovers. Whatever she did, she was discreet. He was the product of two civilized, gracious people.

At an Old Time Fiddlers contest on Mount Lemmon, Jack and Michael volunteered as standby musicians, available as backup for any fiddler needing one. They played for a young contestant, a girl fiddler about seven years old, and Jack thought they'd done exceedingly well, particularly since backup was a relatively unfamiliar genre to each of them.

"Kiddy hoedowns," Michael said, and smoothly danced a clogging step to the exit from the stage.

Jack just bobbed his head a little toward the audience, to indicate good-bye and thanks. He enjoyed the success and hoped the little girl placed high enough to make her happy. She was a cute kid, wearing jeans, a quilted vest over a white shirt, and boots. She was a decent musician, too, and very solemn about it, though he had seen a slight smile when she finished, like she knew she'd done well. He remembered trying to hold a chord on a guitar when the guitar was as big as he was. Someone held it across his lap.

He was surprised when no one else asked him and Michael to provide backup and no one said "good job." He and Michael might as well have been just audience.

Later, Pop Bradshaw walked over to have a cigarette with them and said, "You boys are good. But you sort of drowned out that little girl."

Jack was irritated to hell over that, and then had to admit maybe they were supposed to let the fiddler shine. The kid probably only needed one of them, and they should have toned it down. He wanted the chance to do it over but that didn't happen, since the girl didn't make the finals. He found her with her parents. "You did really well," he said to her, and then looked to the father, engaging eye contact as an apology. "She'll win the next one for sure." He realized he didn't really believe that and added, "Or the one after." It wasn't part of his chosen nature to lie, not even as a compliment. "I think she didn't need so much backup," he said. "She might have done better without us."

"Maybe so. She's not real strong at the mic yet."

Jack accepted that the father had agreed with him. Jack's face flamed but he took the rather gentle rebuke as having been earned.

"She'll do fine." He recognized his father's phrase coming from his mouth. It was a good statement. *You'll do fine. You did fine. You are fine.* His father was a kind man.

After the contest, when the judges gathered to entertain and play for dancing, Pop said, "You boys want to join me for a few tunes?" He cued the keys and chords for each one and Jack and Michael carefully and good-naturedly tried to out-modest each other.

"Mighty fine guitarists," Pop said to the crowd and stepped back for Jack and Michael to do some twin picking. They sang "Redneck Mother," "Up on Cripple Creek," and "Kansas City" and Pop took half breaks behind them. The guy could fiddle anything, just stepped up right on the spot, low-key and smooth. Jack was genuinely appreciative. He'd be slower to judge next time. Maybe not judge at all. It turned into a great day, one he'd remember—up on Mount Lemmon with Pop Bradshaw, snow still clinging to some of the pines. A place with only one road leading to and from it, a snaky road, with drop-offs and scenes worth the risk.

Jack decided the woman Cora might be after him. She always listened to his Kettle sets, and she touched him a lot, just a pat on his shoulder as she went by. He liked that. He liked her smallness, too, and the line of her breasts beneath the silk pink blouse she sometimes wore. The cloth shimmered and slipped with her movements. It was a cheap look but it still drew his eyes. She was about forty. He was a virgin, yes, but not desperate.

"Anytime you need some backup onstage," he said, feeling guilty for thinking of her age, "just tell me. I'll be happy to do it."

"I like my own backup fine, thank you. Anytime you want some harmony, you let *me* know."

He decided he was wrong about her.

Cora

Cora loved The Kettle. It was like a different kind of church, but still a service to God. When she had first moved to the desert country, twenty years ago, she had had a Sears, Roebuck guitar her mother had purchased for her as a birthday gift. It was a three-quarter size, red and black. She had called it Mary, and in her mind thought of it as Mary, Mary, quite contrary. She had a chord book and some beginning songs. The guitar was a miracle compared to the one she had begun with, a battered instrument from an uncle, with the neck so warped that if it'd been a chicken it would have been dead. Pressing the strings down grooved her fingers painfully. Her then husband, a cute man whom she still adored, had disdained musicians, particularly wife musicians and jam sessions. Her mother had taken pity on her and ordered the little guitar.

In the desert country, she discovered that her husband's family included a short guy with a four-string banjo and a fondness for polkas and songs like "Five Foot Two, Eyes of Blue," "Roll Out the Barrel," "Red Roses for a Blue Lady," and "The Naughty Lady of Shady Lane." She learned those songs and others he knew, and at family get-togethers she'd happily join in, though not as gifted as most of them. Sometimes a guest would have a way with a song or an instrument and she'd get a craving and a deep lonesomeness. Most of the time, though, the guitar had languished in a case, brought out on rainy days when she'd been listening to someone like

John Denver sing love, "Annie's Song." Then her husband's cousin began going to a place on Friday nights where musicians gathered. He invited Cora. She rode with him and his wife the first two times.

The Kettle! She wanted to live there! Music spun out of cracks, up through the floor. She ached all over to be able to play as some of those people did. She met a wonderful gal named Amy and another named Susan, and a wickedly hateful one named Bonnie, all of whom were fifteen or more years younger than she, could play snappy and saucy, and had entire lifetimes to make the right choices. They liked her voice, and they wooed her back.

One of the musicians was this big Serbian, maybe twenty-seven, blustery but witty, and light on his feet. When Cora sang "Omie Wise," he came and stood by the older group. When she finished, he got her aside and told her she should sing some Serbian ballads.

"I can't speak Serbian."

"Of course you can't, but you can memorize words. You got the voice for Serbian songs."

His eyes truly smoldered. She told him she liked Norman Blake best, but also Doc Watson. She had discovered Doc Watson years ago.

"You like Doc Watson, you got to like me," he said. "I got a Doc Watson collection that'll blow you away. Nobody's got a collection like I do."

She knew he was exaggerating, but there was the music, and the headiness of being in danger, newly free, and alone. She had moved out of her husband's home and, recently divorced, had a tiny house with a hideous yard and a malfunctioning water heater.

When the last musicians were leaving, the Serbian, Milosh, leaned down to her car window. "You could follow me home, see my record collection."

It was almost a joke, the oldest line, but he was so intense, and sweet, big, dramatic. She had never done anything like that—gone home with a man she barely knew.

"Okay," she said.

He took her hand quickly, kissed the back of it, and said, "Don't get lost."

Those things didn't happen in real life—a hand kiss.

She followed his car, a sturdy new something or other. He drove slowly and used the blinker long before he turned, as if drawing in a lure. She wasn't going to do anything except look at his records.

Only that. She did love Doc Watson, his sound and the people and places he sang about—common and yet grand too. Handsome Molly, Alberta. Matty Groves. And a yodeling gambler. Her dad had yodeled and gambled. His favorite song was "Jole Blon." Cora had loved the bastard.

Milosh lived in a nice neighborhood, a modest stucco house. He showed her the albums and left her sitting on the floor looking through them while he went into the kitchen and started heating water for coffee.

"Find something you want to hear, just let me know," he said.

"Eight of them already."

He came back quickly, took an album from the floor in front of her, slipped the vinyl out and put it on the turntable. It was the one with "Omie Wise." He was by the kitchen stove now, but he was watching her.

She was listening to music and falling in love again. It was supposed to happen only once. If it was real.

She didn't sleep with him, though it would have been so easy to do. He kissed her just before she left. She drove, crying and thinking she might die tonight. She might get paid back for such sharp, sheer, short happiness by dying tonight.

A couple of weeks later, when she was leaving The Kettle early, he followed her outside. "You need someone to take care of you," he said. "Walking outside alone. Bad idea."

"There's a crowd inside. And someone is always outside."

"Yeah, but who? Huh? That's the question."

When she shut the car door—which was so terribly hard to do with him standing there, wooing her, or whatever it was—he put two hands over his heart and started singing. Singing in the parking lot. "'O sole mio," husky and full, followed by the same tone in words she didn't understand but certainly did, too, understand. He stopped singing, not smiling, hands still over his heart.

"You idiot," she said.

"Ah, but you like me." He dropped his hands.

"Yes, I do. But I'm not going to do anything about it."

She drove away. Difficult. Joyous. Heart beating too much. A little breathless.

~:

The door was unlocked, as Milosh had told her it would be. He wasn't there yet. The house had the dry sunniness of an empty southwestern house: tile floors, many windows, pale curtains not fully closed. Vertical light shafts slipped through the room, like departing guests. He had put a bouquet of flowers on the low coffee table. The arrangement was too big for the table, tall, overflowing. He had stuffed the long-stemmed flowers in the vase himself. Droplets of water had dried on the table. The day seemed one from long ago, maybe a time before her own. Another state, even. Another country. Framed, richly colored pictures decorated the little spaces between windows and doors. The people looked like saints or bishops. Maybe they were relatives.

His phone rang, and she didn't know what to do. Answering it could be foolish, but then he could be calling her. They were adults.

She answered it. It was him.

"Making sure you're there," he said. "Don't leave. I'm right around the corner. Got caught in traffic."

Instantly, she wanted to flee, because he shouldn't have phoned. How rude the crash into the moment, him down the street.

He came into the house hurriedly, didn't speak, just drew her up, kissed her gently twice, then again, then kissed her eyelids, pressed her head against his big chest and sighed.

Amy and Carl

Amy had this funny tingling high on her right thigh and even higher, just inside the lips of her private parts. It wasn't exactly a pain, but it wasn't comfortable. She finally had to take a mirror to herself, which she found disgusting. Nothing. Later, though, there was a visible rash and one small blisterlike spot, and she didn't feel well. She was flushed, sort of flulike.

She had never cheated on George, so it couldn't be anything bad, that kind of bad. Still, she waited for George to be in a pretty good mood. They were lying in bed together and he rolled over to bite at her nipple.

"I don't think we'd better do anything," she said.

"Oh?" Mock consternation followed by his best leer. "That time again? Just finished, didn't you?"

"I got this place, an eruption."

Now his eyes narrowed in real concern, but he didn't speak.

"You slept with anyone else, George? Since we been together?"

"Oh no you don't. You get something from messing around and you blame me."

"I haven't been with anyone."

"I'm not the one with a problem."

The windows were gray from the light night sky. The bedroom was cluttered and dirty. "If we're together," Amy said, "how can this be all my problem? I didn't cheat on you."

"I didn't mess around either. But," he admonished her with a shake of his finger, "if it's herpes, you could have got it a long time ago and it's just showing up now." He waited a second, then added, "And it's still your problem. I'm not suffering anything. I don't plan to either."

She bought some over-the-counter ointment, used it and a pleasantly scented lotion, and the itching and burning went away.

George used a rubber for a while and then stopped. She thought his lack of self-protection was a real sign of love for her. It made up for some of his less pleasant ways. She still wondered, though, if he had given something to her and was just pretending to protect himself. She wasn't much for pretense, though she might be, she admitted, thoughtless. Impetuous. She wasn't sure about herself.

～

She met a college dropout, Sally, who could sing and owned a bass, a huge old Kay. They got Bonnie to join them and Amy showed her how to chord a mandolin. "You want to join us?" she asked Cora, knowing the answer beforehand.

"I'm too old for you guys."

"Not so. We could use your voice."

"No. I couldn't keep up."

Cora's insecurity alone would've slowed them down, Amy acknowledged to herself, but she had truly been willing to allow that. "If you ever get ready, we'll add a spot. We're an easy group. No second, dark meaning to that."

Cora laughed with her. Cora liked men, as did Amy, even as friends, and that made for an intuitive friendship. Women could spot it. They weren't hungry women. They were just healthy and fond of the opposite sex.

Amy couldn't contain her delight about her all-girl band.

George didn't like the new situation at all, not at all. "You're cutting me out of music," he said. "Now you'll get gigs for your tits-and-ass group instead of us."

"It's not the same kind of music."

"I'm going to get something going for me, too," he said. "We'll see who plays the most gigs."

He went into his finger-jabbing mode, following her and poking his argument into her flesh. She wheeled around and slapped him hard right on that narrow-angled, glaring face and knew immediately she'd made a mistake. His fist knocked her backward and down. She banged her neck against the coffee table, and his stash spilled. He picked it up calmly. She heard him sit down and knew he was rolling a joint. She didn't really hurt yet, but she was in a distant, dizzy world, like coming off a carousel.

"Got carried away," he said, after she had struggled to a sitting position. He crossed his legs and they hung together like slats of wood. He handed the joint to her. She took a drag she didn't want, because it was the thing to do right now. If she got up, she would have to do something, and she didn't know what it was.

He came to take the joint, sat next to her on the floor. He draped that bone arm across her back. "Sorry, baby. I just don't want to lose you. We got something fine going here, and you keep looking for something else. Hurts me, you know?" He lifted tendrils of her hair, real gently, like she was precious. He kissed her neck. She felt a chill radiate over her shoulders and down her spine. It was painful and delicious. He began unbuttoning her blouse, and she felt that certainly she loved him. But she was still scared to move.

※

"I never hit a woman in my life," Carl Bradshaw said to Amy. He slipped a blank tape in his stereo. "And I don't think much of a man who does."

Amy busied herself tuning for a moment. When she looked

47

up, she said, "Are you going to judge the Safford contest or compete?"

"Judge. I've done my competing. Time for me to work the other end. I take it you don't want to talk about that man of yours."

"Right." She sat on a high stool by the stereo. A dark bruise like a birthmark covered her left cheekbone, temple, and eye. The eye was swollen almost shut, was just a slit that watered. She kept a tissue in her lap and dabbed the eye occasionally. Her lip, too, was swollen, cut nearly through. "He only hit me once," she said. "I hit a table and it made me bite through my lip."

"And that, of course, wasn't his fault," Carl said. "He only came in contact with one spot. So," he put a finger under her chin, "I guess he's only responsible for, say, three inches? Good thing he has small hands."

"Quit looking at me, Pop. I feel stupid enough."

"You don't look stupid. Look hurt. I could talk to him for you."

"We could ride up together and share a room. Cut down on costs."

He gave up. Women talked when they wanted and nothing short of God could make them talk when they didn't want to. "Who you backing up?"

"Paul Welford."

"Then you shouldn't have any costs. He should pay for your room."

"Really?"

"Sure. He wants you along, he pays your way."

"His wife wouldn't like it. And he might get ideas."

"Meaning I wouldn't?"

"You're not married, Pop. You got ideas?"

"I got the idea you shouldn't live with that George fellow." He hurried on. "How come he's not going to the contest?"

48

"He is. I told him I was going by myself this time. We don't have to be a musical team and maybe going separately will prove that."

"Wouldn't have anything to do with his hitting you?"

"Let's do one of your F medleys."

Carl recognized a woman protecting a man in her own way. More power to her, he guessed. Or more pity. He struck up "Oklahoma Rag," went into "Margie," "Sweet Georgia Brown," "Up a Lazy River." She liked the old tunes. Any tune, he guessed.

He had about ten tapes of their jamming together. He taped the conversations too. Some nights, when he felt particularly old and lonesome, he played the tapes and listened to her bright voice and chunky guitar. That quirky laugh, a kind of sweet cackle. She could warm a whole room. Maybe a woman like that could even warm him up. But he wasn't a fool. She didn't see him as a man. She herself was a bit of a slob—he'd been to parties at her house—but she had a good, full heart. She was like a joy sponge, wanting to soak up all the good world. And she was very fond of men. Most women were. Why did they pick the bastards of the world?

⌣⋅

When they drove to Safford together, the bruise was gone and Carl enjoyed the smooth happiness of Amy's pleasant face. She put one tape after another into the cassette deck and would practice dry-run guitar with her nimble fingers. Finally she got her mandolin from the backseat and played along with the tape. She was a natural musician.

The desert spread out black and star-dotted and she filled the car with the pleasure of now. She was something. When they got to the Safford motel, he said, "You want your own room, young lady?"

"Nah. Let's give people something to talk about."

"I'd like to do just that," he said, "with a little bit of encouragement."

"Maybe I better have my own room."

"I'll settle for having you in the other bed. Only to save money, of course."

"Of course."

"But you put some perfume on before you go to bed so I can sort of remember what it could be like."

"I don't wear perfume."

"Soap'll do."

He didn't really want a relationship with a young woman, but he would like to have a full world. A family. People who cared for one another and shared the highs and lows of life. Or at least shared more than surface moments.

She was a good little gal to know. Her singing voice wasn't the truest, but it communicated her feelings about the song and the situation and her mood and everyone liked to hear her. When she hit good licks on the guitar, she wasn't seeing anyone in the audience. There was a spot in the air she focused on. He had one of those spots too. Just sort of found that moment of music and loved it more than anyone else could.

⌣

Amy put her guitar case in the shade, bent down to open it, and heard someone speak right behind her. George.

"I been looking for you," he said. "Thought you'd get in last night."

She stood and turned around. George was all sleeked up, creased jeans, blue shirt, denim vest, bolo tie, and black hat with a turquoise band. He removed his hat as if for her, and twisted it in his hands, like he was insecure. She felt oddly comforted, almost soft toward him, just for looking like that.

With the scent of pine needles all around, the strains of music on the hot air, and him all sheepish and waiting, she wanted to be part of the couple they had been. "We did," she said. "We stayed in a motel in town."

"You and who?"

"Pop Bradshaw. Like I told you."

"Okay." He continued playing with the hat, glancing up to meet her eyes only briefly, then away again. "I wouldn't have blamed you, though, if you'd come with someone else. You know. I guess I sort of asked for it."

"Yep. You asked for it. But I didn't. Just Pop and me."

He touched her cheek with the back of his fingers. "Love you, babe."

"I know, but now I'm scared of you. Can't change that." She knelt by her case, weak with honesty and courage and lonesomeness too. "I don't want to be afraid of anybody."

He squatted next to her and gently capped the back of her head with his left hand. "I'm sorry. Never again." He kissed her ear. "If you'll forgive me, never again."

"I don't know," she said. "Let's talk later. I came to make music. You got your guitar?"

"You bet."

"Who you backing up?"

"Nobody yet. I was thinking maybe I'd join you and Paul. He could use two."

He was changing again. A wiliness had crept in with the music talk. Sure it was true some fiddlers sounded better with two or more accompanying instruments. But Paul didn't want much background when he played, and George knew that. "I guess you could play mandolin," she said.

"I'm not as good on the mandolin as you are. Why don't you do it, and I'll do the guitar."

"But Paul asked *me* to back him up. I don't think he'd like it. You got a different style."

"You don't ever think like a couple, Amy. You're a solo all the way, a me-me-me person." He gave her his sideways look. "You got your own room at the motel?"

She felt unfairly twisted, love me, hate me. "That would be a stupid waste of money. Got my own bed though."

"What if I join you two? I had to sleep in the car last night. A floor might be nicer."

"Nope. It'd look like we set it up all along."

He stalked off, suddenly too lean, in spite of the good clothes. He was wiry and disgusted with her. But wasn't she disgusted with him too? She watched him strike up a conversation with a group of musicians down the road. Then he opened his case and took out his guitar. She couldn't hear the tune, but the fiddler looked pretty pleased with George. That was the way with musicians: find a slot here and there, cut out the weaker guys. Somebody would always have to make way for George. Why was she bullheaded about sharing with him? Maybe she was just a selfish bitch, like he said. She shook her head against that. Today she was going to be happy. Happy, happy.

⌣̣

She loved contests. Loved them. Oh joy day, joy day. Paul Welford's fiddle was singing. Lively, happy bursts over the crowd. *Listen to the mockingbird. T-rrrrr-i-lllll* the strings. *Listen to the mockingbird. Oh the mockingbird is singing in the trees. Trrrrrrilllllll.* "Fire on the Mountain." "Martin's Waltz." Desert fall breeze roaring through the mic, whipping Amy's hair and clothing. George standing just left in front of the stage, looking up at her critically, nodding at the hot passages. People sitting on blankets, in lawn chairs, babies crying, couples dancing in the dust. Tents. Camps. Portable potties. Sun slanting but cool. This was the best life in the world. Tag the waltz, turn around, tag again. Paul was an ass but his fiddling was lovely. He raised his black cowboy hat to the crowd, clicked his heels, and bowed. Amy just ducked her head to the applause. That's what women were supposed to do. She saw George right in front. He gave her an "okay" sign.

Going down the stage steps, she was approached by an obese man with a blue fiddle. "Would you back me up, hon? We got time to run through my tunes."

"Sure."

Another fiddler was right behind him. "How about me, little lady?"

Her hands danced all day.

When the winners were posted, Paul Welford was first, Gary Hargrove's friend second, and the blue fiddler fifth. George's fiddler was way down the list. She was sorry for George, but she didn't say anything.

They jammed late into the night at Welford's campsite. Amy played mandolin part of the time, borrowed a bass for two songs. She sang lustily, drunk on music and a good time. When George stepped forward from the circle, trying to make his lead melody snap them all to attention, she yelled, "Hush, you guys, you're drowning him out," and the other musicians obeyed. They lowered their volume till his precise, careful melody could almost be heard. When he stepped back, they surged loud again.

George led her happy body back into the trees. "Stay with me, baby."

"Nope." Vigorous shake of her head. "I'm staying in Pop's room, just like I said."

"Then I'm staying there too, or we're off. I'm not going to look like a hang-around flunky for you. I got you started in this crowd, you know."

That was true. He had taken her to The Kettle. He had taught her harmony lines. He had gotten her invited to some of the big boys' parties, where only the hot pickers went. She had jammed with Hot Strays, sang with Bill Meister, sat in on gigs with Hiram Betz and Merle Wilson. All because of George. She did owe him, but that wasn't the *whole* truth.

"I'm pretty good by myself," she said.

"We'll just see about that." He shadowed away and left her by this old rough tree to lean against and get dizzy by. She watched the moonlight through baring branches and then curled back to the campsite.

"I don't feel so good," she said to Pop Bradshaw.

"Then we call it a night?"

In their room, the neon light outside flashed against the curtain so she had to close her eyes. She sank down into pleasant-day-done sleepiness.

On his bed, Pop drank a little from a flask in his breast pocket. He undressed to his shorts and undershirt and hung his clothes up carefully. He studied her slight shape on the bed. A happy little gal, that. Enjoyed everything she did. He sat back down, watching her and longing for some kind of longing to overtake him. He thought she might be asleep. But she might be waiting for him to prove his manhood.

"Amy?" he said. No answer. He took another swig from the flask. He wasn't much of a drinking man. His wife had told him he'd never been good in the sack. He had known that before she told him. Men know what they're good at and what they're not. They didn't have much choice in the matter. He would've traded music for a better man's instrument. Maybe. Maybe he would have.

He sat on the edge of Amy's bed and fondled her right breast. She didn't stir. Neither did he. He pressed his lips against hers and she sort of squirmed away with a "Whhaaa" and opened her eyes. "You're cute as a button," he said, and kissed her again. She didn't struggle at all. He sat up.

"I'll get out of my things," she mumbled, and proceeded to sit up and unbutton her blouse. Her dark hair was tousled, her cheeks flushed, and her lips moist. She stood to step out of her skirt and drop it on the floor. Her breasts hung down rich, white, full, with light brownish nipples. A thin line of black hair led from her navel to the fuller hair at her groin. She turned her bare rear end to him while she pulled back the covers. Then she crawled in bed and patted the space next to her.

He removed his shorts but not his undershirt and slipped in beside her. "You got some real pretties," he said. He clutched her right breast and kissed her again, all the while rubbing his parts against her thigh. He realized she wasn't really kissing him back. She was yawning.

"I guess I drank too much," he said.

"Me too."

"Good thing or I'd be taking advantage of you right now."

"Any time, Pop."

She seemed to be waiting and he knew they'd both wait forever, so he patted her shoulder. "I got to judge tomorrow morning. This might be better when we're both sober."

"Might be."

He got into his own bed.

Sometime later, while he was still groggy from beginning sleep, he had to stumble from his bed to answer the door. Her man George stood there, twisting as if from the cold.

"Think I could camp on your floor?" he said. "Temperature's dropped quite a bit."

"I don't think Amy'd like that," Pop said.

"Let me talk to her."

"She's sleeping like a stone."

George creaked around the edge of the door and peeked under Pop's arm. "Okay," he said. He headed back to his Volkswagen.

"I don't care if he stays," Amy said from the bed.

"You don't? Okay then." Pop called to the man outside, "Come on back. I can't sleep in a bed and on the floor too."

He thought they'd probably have the good grace to wait till he was sound asleep to hop on each other's bones, but they didn't. He wondered what it was like to have manhood rise even without will, just lead you to what you wanted. They were a noisy couple, sounded a little like waves slapping on rocks, but even that tide couldn't keep him awake. He was weary and fell into dreams he wouldn't remember in the morning.

Amy

Amy lied to George. "I'm going to practice with the ladies," she said. "Our music would drive you crazy if we did it here."

"All sob ballads. Cry, cry, cry, die, die, die."

"Yep."

"Will you be late?"

"I doubt it."

Then she drove all high from guilt out to Big Bob's party, with the night-cool desert sweeping around her, the car bouncing along the rutted road. Big Bob had asked her not to tell George. She should've said, "Then I won't come either." But she hadn't. She was a selfish woman. She couldn't feel bad though. Her whole being was humming with music and that drowned out everything else.

Winterdog was there, in Bob's long, ramshackle living room, with their banjoist, sweet Davie Moss, driving "Big Sandy" through the walls. Davie fascinated her. He was as short as she, and so white he seemed really vulnerable. Maybe even sunshine could kill him. She didn't know. Behind thick glasses, his pale eyes shivered all the time, and she wanted to look at him until they stilled. She thought that could happen if she were intent enough. Pete and Molly were talking to a fiddler visiting Big Bob. Pete and Molly did Cajun. Pete was an olive-skinned dude with real broad shoulders, black hair, and an angry, bony face. He could play anything okay, but he was best at training Molly. She was blond, tall, and very slender, like a will-o'-the-wisp ghost, and so shy she'd drop her eyes if a fly landed on her. Amy had slept with Pete once a long time ago and he was good. It was like making love to a devil, all intense and silent and angry. That's probably why Molly stayed with him. Everybody knew.

Amy unpacked her guitar and stepped up to Winterdog, tuning as she moved in. She locked on the break a second before Davie moved aside for her. When she finished the break, she stepped back slightly and Davie came forward. She had joined them smoothly and courteously and had not flubbed the opportunity. After the song tagged out, Bob handed her a beer and she took a long swig and then set it at her feet. She undid the top two buttons of her blouse to free her arms.

"Hey girl," Davie said. "We want to keep our mind on the music."

She jiggled her breasts. "What about your hands? They free?"

He ran a scale up the banjo neck while he looked at her. "You bet. Free and fast."

She just did fill runs on the next two tunes to make up for being pushy.

"You've really come along," Davie said at some point and she nodded like the men always did. It had taken her a long time to learn the right language. She could have said, "Thanks" or "Thank you kindly" but nothing more or she wouldn't yet be good enough. You weren't good just because your music was hot. You had to know the game.

When Davie took a beer out to the wraparound, screened-in porch, she followed him. It was a little chilly out there, but pleasant, the winter desert softened by moonlight. "Where you guys playing now?"

"We split a weekend gig with Pete and Molly, down at Sonoita, The Horseshoe. Cajun one weekend, bluegrass the next. You ought to come down."

"I'd like to."

"You could sit in on a set."

She almost said, "You're kidding," but caught herself. "Might do that." She chewed her thumbnail from the contained joy. She thought his stubby white fingers were endearing, and his reddish ears. "I've never heard anyone who could beat you on the banjo," she said, "and never expect to." She stood before he could answer, very matter-of-factly. "I'm going in, see if I can do some Cajun bass." What if it wasn't her music he liked? She wasn't going to think about it. He'd invited her and she would, by damn, play with them.

She forgot to worry about George until the party was over. The road to the highway was all dirt and snaked through the desert a long time. George could be somewhere on this road. Spying. What if she saw his car parked along here, waiting to prove her deception? She hummed "Georgia Pines" and tapped the steering wheel. What if George had heard about the party from someone else? He'd make her pay. Her pleasure in the evening was being worried away. That itself was a huge payment.

At home, George was watching television. "How'd it go?" he said.

"Okay. Some tight harmony."

Something in the way he watched her, maybe the twisting of his moustache or the twitching of his feet on the coffee table, clued her in. He knew or suspected.

"You watch television all evening?" she asked.

"No. Big Bob had an impromptu and I went out there for a couple of hours."

She felt the burn in her cheeks. "Shit," she said. "Why didn't he tell me?"

"You weren't here and I didn't know where you were practicing."

This was a new kind of lying, sort of a master lie. George was claiming to have been at a party she'd just left. "Who all was there?"

"Winterdog, Pete and Molly, William Cullen, that Canadian guy."

He had heard about it for sure. "Damn!" she said, and almost added, "You could've come looking for me." But at the last moment she caught herself. What if he had?

"What about Pop Bradshaw? He there?"

"Nope."

He was studying the television now, but his feet were still twitching and his mouth too. He was a live wire holding still.

"Sorry I missed it," she said.

"Yeah."

She expected a blow, or a blowup, some kind of fearful explosion, but he went to bed in his silent wrath and finally she followed him. His nonsleep weighted the bedroom. She couldn't understand. Then she stumbled on the reason, maybe the reason. He couldn't rage at not being invited because that made it real and worse. The lie let her be the one excluded and him the one invited. It was false but still the only reality they had acknowledged, so in a way it was real. The whole idea hurt her head, but she knew she was right. Now she had to feel sorry for him in a different way, deeper, more whole, for a trapped person.

Cora

Cora waited at a table near the stage for Milosh. The candles in their red bowls made The Kettle look Italian or somehow foreign and wonderful. She sat so she could see the entryway without having to turn but wasn't truly facing it. Musicians nodded hello, but went through the double doors to their right and the jamming room beyond. Her guitar was in there. She wanted to watch a couple of acts first and then jam. She usually did her duty as audience later in the evening, after she'd played and eased her excitement. She wanted so much, so deep it hurt, to be a musician and not just part of an audience. Her place in the music world was tenuous. She understood her position. If she could live her life over, she'd beg everyone in her little hometown for a piano. She wouldn't quit. She'd pray for one. Maybe she *had* done that. She didn't recall much of her childhood faith.

Now, guarding her newborn happiness with restraint, she heard Milosh's voice and raised her eyes.

He had spotted her and was holding the gaze a moment, but a small woman was to his left and his arm was down, hand behind her, as if lightly guiding her into the room. The woman looked at Cora. They both knew, Cora supposed. Cora nodded as if just acknowledging an entering guest, and scooted her chair, the legs scraping loudly and ridiculously on the wooden floor. No grace there. Her eyes had flooded but she didn't have a purse with her and didn't carry tissues in her jeans pocket. A tiny message tried to grow big, *He's with a relative from the old country. It's a cousin, a friend's wife*, but her whole body knew differently. This was pain earned by a foolish woman. Endure it.

Someone was joining her. A tear-blurred Amy. "He's an asshole," her friend said. "But I know how you feel. Let's go jam."

"In a few minutes." When the act ended, Cora stood up and, with Amy beside her, walked toward the back room without looking at the tables. She knew Milosh was there, though, with that black-haired someone. Their table might as well have been the dark side of the moon.

He brought the woman into the jamming room shortly, determined, Cora guessed, to have his new companion or sweetheart or whatever acknowledged. Cora stopped playing and met the woman's gaze. She had hot eyes, sharp, not unkind.

Amy kept tuning while the names went around, but she bobbed a quick recognition and glanced at Cora, still easing the note into place.

"It's all right," Cora said, watching Milosh sliding off with his prize. He loved women. He happened to look back just then with a sheepish guilty happiness on his face.

"I wish he hurt a little," she said to Amy. "Maybe he will."

Even though she hurt as well, she didn't mean that. She didn't want him to hurt. Idiot Serb. Crazy kind of male. All bluster and romance. She felt her eyes watering up. "Shit," she said.

Amy laughed. "Good girl!"

Carl

One of the neighborhood women, Callie, introduced herself to Carl by showing up at his door one Sunday with a chuck roast on a platter, brown and steaming the plastic wrap to a close fit.

"I noticed you live alone and I thought you might like a home-cooked meal."

She came in for a while and he served coffee and offered her part of the roast.

"I've already eaten. That's for you. You don't have to have any now. Just when you want it."

She was somewhere between sixty and seventy, but well preserved, her skin pale and delicate. She wore a little blue shadow above the eyes and a blotted-out red on the lips. Her nails were cut short and buffed but not polished. She wore real pretty shoes.

It was a good roast, cooked to fall-apart tender and lightly salted. He ate a lot to show her how very good it was.

"I've always wanted to be musical," she said, glancing at the work counter he'd fashioned on one side of the kitchen. "I hear you playing every now and then. You give lessons?"

"Nope."

"I thought if you did, I might take something up."

"Any instrument in mind?"

"You play the fiddle, don't you?"

"Yep."

"You have to be young to start out?"

"Helps. Helps with anything."

She smiled. "I'm a hard worker and persistent. I'll learn at least a few songs."

"I'm not a real teacher," he said. "I can only teach by playing along, but I can't seem to get anyone started from scratch. Don't know why that is."

He loaned her an old fiddle and brought her an instruction book from the Emporium. He thought she'd be asking him to tune it every day, but she only waved at him if they happened to be outside at the same time. When she came by his place to play her first tune, she said, "It's not nearly as hard as I thought. I know I don't sound real good yet, but I never thought I'd be able to do even this much."

He got out his fiddle and played a standard "Old Joe Clark" with her, single slow notes, five times in a row. Then he couldn't control himself and he whipped into double-time, double-stop shuffles, turnaround, tag and out. "Way some people play it," he said, "after they know it pretty well." He put his fiddle on the workbench. "Of course, it takes some practice."

He didn't really like people who thought they were better than they were. It was fine to play lousy as long as you had a little humility. A good spirit sweetened the sound.

The next few hours he was disgusted with himself. Why did he judge Callie so harshly? She just wanted something she didn't have. The desire alone was admirable, wasn't it? What if she proved him wrong and turned into a fine fiddler? What if? He made a kind of harrumphing sound. He knew what he knew and didn't want to own up to it.

She was a new kind of woman for him. He'd heard about them, and seen them. They could handle anything.

⌣

Some dark-haired woman knocked on Carl's door after midnight, when he had to go to work the next morning.

"Jesus took the skillet and threw it in your yard," she said. She was a squirrel woman, quick eyes, pointed face, about thirty-five and a little plump. She went back down the steps and said, "See? Look here? All over the whole goddamned place."

Two black skillets were in his yard, one on a dead tree stump and the other just sitting in the dirt. He went to the bedroom to put on a shirt. When he returned, the woman was gone but the skillets weren't. He had a cigarette, sitting on the arm of his sofa and waiting for something to happen. Finally he went back to bed for a little more sleep before work. That evening, when he came home from the Emporium, the skillets were still there. He decided taking them to her might be somewhat hazardous. Moving them at all might be removing an anchor she needed for her craziness. The next morning there were plates and silverware in his yard, too, but he didn't want to be late for work. It looked like she was moving her kitchen into the out-of-doors. Or—wait a minute—into his territory.

Callie the fiddle-lady neighbor appeared shortly after he came home that evening. "We really had a mess here today," she said. "You know that woman who lives two houses down from me? Dolores Nelson? We had to call the authorities. She went clear out of her head."

"Who's 'we'?" Carl said. It seemed a pity that a whole troop of people had to turn on one sad crazy lady.

Later, almost dozing in his chair, a sound startled him and he realized he feared someone was at his door again.

⌇

Carl missed Oklahoma. He missed the storms that raged through and uprooted trees and shook houses and occasionally took a whole house. He missed everything, mostly what he'd never had. A house with a loving woman had a presence all its own. He knew when he was in such a place, because that's what his parents had had. No money. No education. Probably no social graces. Every chair had a slipcover made from material on sale; every chair had a peculiar sag. The curtains were homemade. Nothing matched. The pine floors were too loose to hold varnish and too used to hold polish. Rag rugs here and there warmed him as he crossed the floor on early winter mornings. Some weeks the main meals were fried baloney or just beans and corn bread. But his parents were each other's, and the house was scented with that. Belle and Jim Bradshaw. Country people.

Carl hadn't married till he was almost thirty. He'd lived alone, but spent most of his daytime working with his dad or for other farmers, doing some repair work on the side, and playing music with his buddies. A good life, he recalled. The woman he married had been younger than he was in years, but far ahead of him in other ways. He hadn't known that then. She was tiny, witty, and loved to dance. He'd first seen her on the dance floor, being waltzed around and spun by another man. Somehow, she kept winding up right in front of the band, watching Carl over the other guy's shoulder. One night she danced by herself. He had led into "Milk Cow Blues," and she came onto the dance floor straightway. Women occasionally danced together or would at least get on the dance floor together and do their best moves alone, dancing for the men a little shyly, and often awkwardly. "Milk Cow Blues" was a popular couple's dance though. No one else got up. She might as well have had a marquee floating above her. She didn't strip or make one ugly move. She just had the blues rhythm in her body and danced in a small floor space like she was thinking of someone.

The guitar backup exhaled heavily and said, only for Carl, "Damn, does she want you."

Well, she had him. From that moment. He wanted that woman. He thought maybe he had been waiting on a woman like her, was meant for her. The thought of her ate him up inside. There wasn't another one in the world.

He squired her around in his old pickup. The seats were cracked, the stuffing poked out. She didn't complain, but on a few dates she brought a paper sack to cover the seat. He taped the cracks up, then tried a seat cover. She didn't seem to want much, just to be dancing or to be naked and making love. He was certainly willing. He'd been more of a man then, able to satisfy them both, though he was only good for one go at a time. "You'll get over that," she said. She liked being the lead fiddler's girl, sitting at the band's table. Soon she wanted to try singing with the band. The guys let her do a couple of vocals, but her voice was too sharp. No feeling to it, except maybe desire and anger. Since she couldn't sing with them, she danced every song with some man in the crowd. Men were always dogging around her, which Carl understood. "I'm not going to sit like a damned log while you're onstage," she said.

He married her, thinking that would contain her and free him. The contempt the marriage brought out in her spread throughout the house like smoking trash. He didn't know why she had married him, unless she was trying to escape herself, or wanted to make a man feel ashamed. He took a full-time job repairing instruments, played steady gigs, and took on farmwork when it and he were both available. Whatever she wanted, he bought when he could. It wasn't enough. She took to parading around the house naked, any time of day. He assumed if someone knocked, she would open the door like that. The more she flaunted her sexuality, the stiller his manhood got. That was a double shame to him.

The week before she told him she was filing for divorce, she had pulled back the covers one night, pulled his shorts down, and put a warm washcloth on him. Then she covered him with her mouth for a few minutes, like she'd draw him up. He shriveled with disgust for her and him too. He wasn't crude enough for her.

Thinking about her now was no good. Made present life full of past pain, and that was a fool's choice.

So he made his little rented Tucson box house as much a home as he could. He kept current magazines by his reading chair, some plastic flowers in a vase on the kitchen table. His dish towels were bleached white, one hanging ready from a cabinet knob. He passed word of an open invitation to his place on Sunday afternoons and some musicians were happy to feel welcome. Michael Halloran wanted to learn Texas backup and he'd ask for a particular song he'd heard Carl do. Halloran had an ear for chord change and his long delicate fingers were surprisingly strong. He could do full-chord backup on a new tune pretty quickly. When Gary Hargrove came, he always had a dish from his wife. He and Carl might have a piece of pie or a saucer of potato salad and then play tunes like "Sail Away Ladies," "Maggie," "Can I Sleep in Your Barn Tonight Mister." Hargrove, from a poor rural life in Missouri, knew a lot of sad country ballads but he liked best the slightly risqué tunes from old years, like "Roll Me Over in the Clover" and "Redhead from Seattle." Cora came by, usually with Amy. Amy, though, was the most frequent visitor. Sweet, happy-natured thing she was. Way too young for an old coot like him. Maybe he had a father's affection. How would he know, never having been a father?

Some Sunday mornings, Carl sat down at the used desk he'd found for twenty dollars and called a few friends in Oklahoma. He smoked and drank coffee and talked as slowly as if he were in their kitchens.

They all missed him, they said, and he grunted his appreciation each time. "Lots of music here, too, like the air breeds musicians, all sizes, all kinds. Not much of that noise music, which makes life a little more pleasant."

Occasionally he heard about Elizabeth and acted only mildly interested. She and Tucker were still together. He wished a person could wipe out past mistakes, could have a chance to redeem himself. He cringed at the kind of man he was. But he'd done himself in by choosing her in the first place. Cringing was natural payment, part of being human.

He thought about calling Billy Wilcox, so the man could come through here if he wished, but he kept putting it off. It was like asking Wilcox not to let the old ties fall away. Sometimes it was best that they did fall away. If he was going to build jealousy from visits, then he should kiss them good-bye.

Mornings were becoming increasingly difficult for him, having to realize each time that he was an old man. Dust in the Tucson sun sometimes seemed like loneliness in action, floating through his house. He reminded himself that he had always wanted to go somewhere, and now he had. He hadn't run away. He had run *to*. It was up to him to be happy.

SET II

TUCSON MEET YOURSELF

From Friday 4:00 p.m. to Sunday 4:00 p.m.
(Closed from 11:00 p.m. each evening till
8:00 a.m. the next morning)
35 Food Booths
Come taste the ethnic cuisine of the Southwest!
Come see the dancers!

CELTIC, INDIAN, MEXICAN, ZYDECO,
WESTERN, SQUARE, AND CONTRA
Come LISTEN!

40 acts scheduled for the main stage
80 acts scheduled for the small stages

Saturday Workshops (see schedule)
Old Time Fiddling
Bluegrass Fiddling
Mandolin
Clawhammer Banjo
Bluegrass Banjo
Flat-Pick Guitar
Backup Guitar (Texas Swing, Old Time, Bluegrass)

Gospel Harmony

Amy

They got started to Sonoita late because Amy couldn't find her blue velvet vest and when she did, it was so crumpled she had to throw it in the dryer with a wet washcloth and then had to iron it anyhow. All the while, George, in his silent sneaking-out-the-truth mood, watched her and asked questions like they were innocent conversation. "Why are you so worried about what you wear?" "Isn't that your contest vest? Thought you wore that just for good luck." "You talk to Davie lately?" "How do you know they're drawing a big crowd?" "So now the lady's ironing. My, my. There's a devil in the woodpile."

She responded in her flustered female way, about trying to change her ways, be neater, slimmer. When she finally looked acceptable to herself, she turned in a full circle for him, pressed against him, and pouted a kiss onto his thin lips. "Now isn't this worth the wait?"

"If we're going, let's hit the road."

Then came his stillness, his aha! look when she picked up her guitar case.

"You planning on playing somewhere?"

"Maybe we'll jam afterward."

"Yeah. That *is* a long way to go just to listen, isn't it?"

His eyes were searching her face, and she assumed her lie was shining in red cheeks and evasive eyes. "Not if you're supporting friends," she said.

"Like Winterdog'd come listen to us if it was the other way round. If it was our gig."

73

"They would. Probably."

"Uh-huh. Sure." He wiped his moustache quickly, a gesture she once found cute. "Particularly if somebody asked them just right."

He grabbed his own case and went out the door first.

Then came fifty miles of speeding down the divided highway, through the lower night, with the false light of city reflected against the sky, a few cars slicing by; then the turn-off into dark hills and a winding, narrow two-lane road, so the car was too slow up, and up, but there, finally, open sky with stars splattered like they had just exploded into view. She was breathless, partly from excitement, partly from guilt, and partly because it was her nature. Life had moments of perfect beauty—the highest reach, the clearest note—and such surprises, over and over, were worth any little discomfort with George or anything else.

She felt sorry for George. He was like a burning wire twisting on itself.

"Why are you always mad at me?" she blurted. "Why can't you just like me?" She'd rarely said anything so personal to him, and it seemed to stir him up. He glanced at her twice.

"You really want to know?"

"Yes, I do. You're always angry. It's like you're out to get me for something and I haven't done anything."

"It's because I can't trust you. You're sneaky. You find ways to trick me and still feel good about it."

"Maybe I have to be sneaky because you won't let me be who I am. You think you have the right to say no to me."

"I do have that right. And you do too. I try pretty much to please you all the time."

"I don't ask you for anything. Tell me one thing I've wanted."

"You want me not to complain about the house, about how late you are all the time. You want me to compliment your guitar playing and the way you look. You want me to be careful with your feelings and I am. I'm being careful right now."

"I'm careful with your feelings too."

"What do you hold back, babe? Give it to me."

"You're too tight. Too severe. You can't loosen up."

"Ha. If you're talking about bed, sweetie, I know you're wrong."

"I'm talking about life. About me. About music." There. She'd done it. She'd come close, at least.

Silence, which she hated, but she knew he needed it. This he was processing, mulling.

"You're saying there's no life in my music. Is that it?"

"You don't ever want to play alone, and you don't want me to play alone. Why is that?"

"Answer my question first."

"I did."

"Like hell."

They were descending into the Sonoita valley, toward the sparse, scattered lights of the old farming and mining communities. She felt lonesome for families, everybody's family. Her body was lonesome. George wasn't hers and she wasn't George's, though how that came about eluded her. She sighed. "I like your music, George," she said. "But I like mine best and you won't let me have it."

They were at the bottom, at the first nonsense stop sign—because there was never any traffic.

"I know what's up," he said. "You got some deal going with Winterdog and you've cut me out."

"I don't have a deal with anyone."

"Why didn't you just come down by yourself?"

"When I said I was going, you assumed you were coming too. Didn't you?"

"You could've told me no."

"You've hit me, George. I remember that even if you don't. I don't provoke you more than I have to."

Now he was quiet, and The Horseshoe lot was in sight, and everything had been smudged ugly and she was both at fault and not at fault. She got out of the car in the Sonoita valley wind, which forever blew, though she didn't understand how that could happen in a valley. "Let's leave the guitars in the trunk," she said.

He didn't answer. He strode ahead of her, pausing just to light a cigarette as if he had to enter with one in his hand. He was a skinny, mustachioed cowboy, with a decent guitar style and hateful ways. She was no great shakes herself. A big bosom couldn't make up for all her flaws, and she wouldn't want it to. He liked more of her than just her breasts. She shuffled after him, and thought briefly of Indian wives, who supposedly accepted beatings because their men deserved some power. It was a sign of passion on each side, the giver and the taker. But she wasn't a wife and she didn't like men who drove women down for any reason. Her dad was a sweet, gentle man. He still called her Cutie. And she could, by God, play better than George. Was knowing that a fault? She wanted to be loved simultaneously as a musician and a woman. She was one package!

The place was packed, smoke thick from the ceiling to the tables, the crowd boisterous, the small dance floor filled. Davie waved from the stage and some people turned to look. Amy found a tiny square table behind a post and sat down, scooting her chair backward till she could see the band. On the other side, George did the same. His left hand tapped a book of matches on the table. She refused to think about his tenseness. She listened. She wrapped herself in sound and delight at the crowd's delight. She thought music even had a scent. She could breathe it in and it filled her to her fingertips and toes.

She and George had two beers each before the break, and when Davie headed their way, pausing occasionally to talk with a fan, she tried to get ready. She just wanted to play. That was all. Just one song, even.

Davie shook George's hand, accepted a cigarette.

"Nice turnout," George said. "You always draw this many?"

"Have been for the last six or so weeks. We have our regulars now. And some of Pete and Molly's people like us too. Gives us two communities, I guess." His pink eyes wavered toward Amy. "How you doing?"

"Great. Got better after I heard you all. You should cut an album."

"We're working on that. Already have a demo tape out. You bring your guitar?"

"Yep."

"You want to join us for a couple of songs?"

He hadn't looked at George. "I don't know," she said. "You got this crowd pretty hot."

"Best time in the world to join us. You do 'Limehouse Blues,' don't you?"

"Yeah."

"And 'Jerusalem Ridge'?"

"Yep."

"Okay. I'll tell the guys. We'll do a couple of songs, then announce you."

"Whenever."

"If it stays good, maybe you can play out the rest of the set with us. We'll see."

He nodded at George. "See you later." He wandered off to visit other tables like entertainers were supposed to do. A short, red-haired girl stopped him, all animated, hugging herself so her breasts pushed up.

"Guess we know what she wants," Amy said, but George wasn't going to let it go.

"He asked you right in front of me. Do you know how that makes me feel?"

"I can't help it."

"You could've suggested we both go up."

"You know I couldn't do that. The invitation has to come

from him." She stood. "I'd better get tuned. Let me have the keys."

George didn't answer. He was up, shoving at his chair, and slinking George-fashion past the scattered tables toward the front door. She followed him outside.

"Don't make trouble, George," she said to his back.

He pulled out the keys, opened the trunk, and took out both cases. "We could tune right here," he said.

"You know he didn't include you. Don't push it. It's their gig."

"Davie's a chickenshit. All of them are." He lifted out the guitar and tuner. "Better get moving."

He looked off as if at the road back to Tucson. She knew all his little signs of control.

"Okay," she said. "I won't go up. It's no big thing."

He was fixed on her now, staring down, weasel face, pale skin, black eyebrows, that humongous moustache.

"I'm actually a better picker than you," he said. "Do you know that?"

She nodded. "In a way you are. I just got punch. Audiences like me because I bounce around a lot and have fun. I surprise them. But I'm good too."

"Not that good. It'd be different if you were. And you know what else? I wouldn't have accepted if he'd asked me and not you."

She didn't know if that was true or not, and she couldn't really care. She wanted to play, right now, more than she'd ever wanted to play. At least it seemed that way. But George was really hurting. If she had any kindness at all, she'd have to deal with that. Surely his feelings mattered more than playing this one night. She had her hands in her pockets as she rocked on her heels. "Let's go on home," she said. "I'll tell Davie later that my E string was broken and I didn't have a spare. I'll make up something."

"You're good at that." George seemed to consider her

suggestion. From inside came the ring of Davie's banjo, and the drive of a fiddle into "Gold Rush." George turned toward the sound, glanced at the neon sign. Then he returned to tuning. "We can split the breaks," he said. "You give me a nod."

"Don't do this, George."

"I'm going up whether you do or not."

She had lost. "I'll tune inside," she said.

George waited at their table, his guitar case beside him. She went into the ladies' room. "Well, old gal," she said to herself in the mirror. "You got yourself in a tight little fix." She could hear the muted music from the band. The door opened and the sound rushed in with the short, red-haired girl, who mussed with her hair before going into a stall. Amy tuned to the song the band was playing, picked along with them. The redhead emerged, rinsed her hands, and dried them with too many paper towels. She was looking at the condom vending machine.

"Good music," Amy said.

The other girl nodded. "The banjo player's named Davie. The albino."

"You know him, do you?"

"He plays here a lot." She was out the door with a young twist.

As Amy practiced, she watched her fingers in the mirror. They fascinated her, like they knew the notes independently of her.

"Get your ass out here," George said from the cracked-open door.

She went up right behind him and quickly noted the looks among Winterdog. She couldn't shrug or anything without it being a betrayal of George.

Davie nodded her to the mic. "Jerusalem Ridge," she said. She bowed her head. An A minor lightning bass to D minor, A minor, C, A minor, E. *DAdadadaDA, DAda DAdaDAda*

79

DAdaDAdaaaaaa, DAdadadadaaaaa, DAdaDAAAAAdadaDA . . .
DA AAAdaDA, dadadAdAdA dadadadadada, dadada DADA . . .
dadadadadadada. Again.

Then George stepped up, a cue that his break was next. She moved aside, began a solid rhythm. "Take it, George," she said, smoothing the transition as best she could, as if this were all planned.

He ruined it, turned a shotgun song into dribbled pellets. She knew the audience noticed. Anyone would, just like they'd notice the slight change in sunlight if a flimsy cloud passed above. She was sorry for George, but ashamed too.

Dadadadadadadadadadadadadadadadadadadadadada . . . dadada
dada, Da . . . dadadadadadadadadadadadadadadada . . . dada
dadada . . . dadadadadadada.

Davie's banjo rang through another microphone. He had taken over the lead, and, with a quick nod, indicated this was the last time through. He repeated the tag four times and out. They ended crisply and together.

"Thank you, Amy Chandler and George Dey," Davie said, facing the audience. "Thank you kindly." He applauded too, a cue that the guest spot was over and she and George were to leave the stage.

Amy felt apologetic throughout her whole body, but she smiled and bobbed her head to Davie and the audience. A one-song sit-in was an embarrassment. Any bluegrass audience would know *that* too.

She headed back to her table, trying to keep a smile on her face. A man caught her wrist briefly and said, "You can really play, girl. Why don't you get back up there?"

"Thanks," she replied, "but we only planned the one song this time." She was grateful to him and to a few people who smiled, said a good word. She was going to let herself feel good. Yes, she was. She wasn't going to be mad at George. That would only make the bad time last longer. Surely he knew how he sounded, what he'd done. But when she sat down, she had difficulty breathing just from trying not to cry or to snap at George.

"I'm going to put my guitar away," George said.

"You should sit down for a song or two," she said. "It won't look right if you miss part of their set."

"Well tough shit. Who gives a good goddamn?" He stalked toward the exit.

Amy ordered a margarita.

George didn't return. When she'd had the second margarita, she walked to the front door and peered out into the lot. His car was gone.

"Down and out in Sonoita, Arizona," she muttered. "Blue and alone."

Davie came to her table during the next break. "George took off?"

"Yep."

"You ready for 'Limehouse Blues'?"

Loyalty to George tugged at her momentarily, but Davie's judgment had been right. She couldn't blame him. "I'm ready for anything," she said.

His hesitation clued her in to the statement's double meaning. "I'll see what I can think up," he said, trailing a finger around the corner of the table. The gesture gave her goose bumps.

She did three songs with them. Then she leaned close to the mic and said, "Enough for me. I sure had fun." She waved a fist above her head. "Thank you all."

"That was Amy Chandler, folks, from Tucson. Hottest little gal around."

⌣

She rode home in Winterdog's van. The guys had built two wood-framed half beds in the back, with storage beneath. The bass hung inches from the ceiling, held by broad leather straps. Amy and three of the guys sat on the beds. When Davie passed her a joint, she took a small hit. She didn't want to get too lost with three men. She wasn't a fool. But they talked mostly music, about the high points of the evening.

"You can sit in anytime you want," Davie said, and the other two nodded.

"But don't bring George. He's a nice guy, but—you know."

"Yeah, I know," she said. "But he's technically good. He taught me a lot."

Davie snorted. "Ah, come on. You got him beat so many ways it isn't funny."

She felt stubbornly defensive about George, and precisely because what they said was true. She owed him something. "George is okay," she insisted. "There's room in music for all kinds. He's just not your kind of musician."

And surprisingly to her, they liked her support of George. She'd passed another kind of test, she guessed. Men were strange creatures.

Davie asked to take the van home and he dropped the other guys off. Then he drove to Gates Pass, on the crest of the Tucson Mountains. He left the back doors open and the sky was right there, all Amy could see, twinkling lights on black, and the music seemed to come from there instead of from the tape deck. They made love on one of the beds. Davie, naked, was so white that it was like making love with a magic elf. But he was firm enough where it counted. He wasn't George though. Davie was softer, shorter, heavier, with small hands, all of which made her feel less womanly. He couldn't take control. George was angles, angry, forceful, and he treated her like she was his. Now, she couldn't come, but pretended to as Davie did. For a while his breathing was fast, then it slowed and his weight became uncomfortable to bear. Was he sleeping on top of her?

"I can't breathe," she said. "Davie."

He rolled to his side, his arm like a ghost's across her stomach.

"You're good at this too," he said. "Thought you might be."

Then, suddenly, she remembered the rash she'd had. She plucked at the bedding. She should have asked him to use something. For both their sakes. "I guess you get a lot of women with that banjo of yours," she said, her voice huskily pleasant even to her own ears.

"Not really," he said. "Most of them are pretty stupid."

She wished he hadn't said that, even though she understood he wasn't referring to her. Or maybe he was. She thought about George, maybe waiting for her at home, and a weakness took over her limbs. Was it fear or lonesomeness? She didn't know.

"I guess me and George are over," she said.

"Because of this?"

"Nah. Lots of reasons."

"Not because of me?"

"No." She knew what he was getting at. This was a one-time thing. She wasn't supposed to count on him. "Of course not." She slapped his hand as if he were silly.

Amy had Davie drive her to Cora's house. It was in an old, poor neighborhood not yet redeemed by the new gentry, and had few streetlights. The stucco houses were white though, and had a soft shine to them even now. Davie stayed in the vehicle but he didn't drive away while she rapped on the wooden screen door. Cora was there in seconds and saw Davie driving off.

"Oh, honey," she said.

Amy was real sad and Cora sat up with her while dawn came. Amy ran through the music part of the evening with George. "I should've protected his image. I knew I was going to play with them. I could have warned him or I could have told Davie that he had to ask George too."

"I'm not sure how all that works," Cora said. "But doesn't George know? He knew he wasn't invited."

"I guess so. But he doesn't know why he's not included. I'm not sure myself."

Amy knew she had lied the moment the words were uttered and expected Cora's response.

"Yes, you are. Even I can tell."

"Well, he can't help it," Amy said, and thought about how he practiced. She felt he had been cheated. And now cheated by her too.

Amy showered and shampooed in Cora's tiny bathroom and used the detachable showerhead to rinse the tub. Then she sprinkled scouring powder on the bottom of the tub and after a minute or so, rinsed that down the drain. She felt a little cleaner.

Cora had fixed breakfast. Amy had never eaten at Cora's house. She had never eaten breakfast in another woman's house. It was odd, a kind of standard life she had missed. She liked eggs over easy and that's how Cora had fixed them.

When she phoned her place and George didn't answer, she had Cora take her over there. George was home after all.

"We can't live together anymore," Amy said. "It's not working out."

He was smoking a cigarette, slumped all slinky in a deep, blue chair by the window. A filled ashtray rested on the arm. "I guess," he grunted, "you're in with the big boys now, if you call that white paste a big boy."

"I'm not 'in' with anybody. Not even you." She stayed near the door. "I don't want to be afraid, George. You scare me when you're mad."

"Then don't ask for it."

"I don't. This is my place, you know. I pay the rent, and I want to live here alone."

He exhaled gray smoke, touched his tongue as if removing a piece of tobacco. "Nobody will want to share this dump with you. But you don't want me? Okay, babe." He stood up, poked that skinny finger like he'd jab her to hell if he could. "You got it."

"Cora's on the front porch," she said.

She'd never know if he planned to hurt her or not, because that shifted him. He stood stock-still, then crunched his cigarette into the ashtray so hard the whole thing fell on the floor. Cora opened the front door. "Everything okay?"

"Yeah," Amy said. "Come on in."

Cora said, "Hi George," as he passed her. Then she got a broom and swept up the ashes, and she and Amy kept silent, just exchanged looks, while George came through the living room carrying armloads of stuff. When he took his guitar, Amy thought he'd have a parting word, but he didn't. She went out on the porch and said, "George." He didn't respond. He spun his little Volkswagen out the other side of the gravel circle and zoomed down the road.

"That guy scares the dickens out of me," Cora said.

"Me too. Sometimes."

Then Cora washed Amy's dishes while Amy sat on the sofa and cried.

Two days later, after work, Amy found all her tires slashed. When she finally got home, down the cost of four tires, with her whole body heat-flushed, she walked into a ravaged dwelling. Windows broken, shaving cream on clothing, food from the refrigerator dumped on her bed. She hurried to her guitar case, saw the damp stain and smelled it at the same time. She jerked up the top. The Martin was untouched. She sat back on her heels, grateful. He had urinated on the case, but only the case.

She knew George was the culprit, though she couldn't prove it. She was glad in a way, because somehow it evened them up.

·.·

On a Friday at The Kettle, George got onstage with a girl in her twenties, whose skin was rough and flushed, but whose voice was powerful and true. She sang "W-o-m-a-n," "How Mountain Girls Can Love," and a cowgirl song about a lover on a lonesome prairie. George seemed a little ravaged himself, even bonier, and his eyes were set deeper. Maybe he had truly loved her. Amy had a deep longing to still be in love with George and wondered why there wasn't much difference between aching to love and being in love.

Amy's women's group did a guest set at The Horseshoe, then got a gig at the Hilton for Wednesday's happy hour.

The Kettle

A new man appeared at The Kettle. He drew looks like the devil had popped up amid the musicians. He was smallish, about 5'6", though he later told someone he was 5'10", which at first caused guffaws and then concessions that maybe he *had* been that tall. He seemed liked a big man. He had thick straight hair, just long enough to reach an inch past the top of his collar. The hair was shoe-polish black, no sheen to it at all, but slick and always perfectly in place. He was a little portly in the belly, wore a black suit, wrinkled and apparently comfortable, a white shirt, and boots with at least two-inch heels. He seemed simultaneously stylish and unpretentious, like he set standards. He wasn't a pushy man though. He stood outside different groups, real appreciative, but he didn't ask to borrow anyone's instrument. Everybody knew he was a musician. They wondered what instrument.

"What do you play?" a mandolin player asked him.

"Little bit of everything, not much of anything."

"You want to sit in for a few minutes?"

"No. You guys put me to shame. I'll listen." He smiled and turned his gaze first here, then there, like he could hear all the songs at once and individually too. In one group, someone fiddled "The Devil's Dream," a mandolin whipped "Don't Let Your Deal Go Down," Gary Hargrove sang "Up a Lazy River," and Milosh Lukovich tried to fiddle a blues turnaround for "Milk Cow Blues." A kid seated on the floor tried to tune his new guitar and look like a polished, bored musician as he did so.

"Anyone here know the old version of 'Little Flora'?" Big Bob Burden asked.

The stranger raised his hand, as if waving a casual hello. "I can sing it," he said.

"So can I."

"Then you go ahead, sir."

The words were gentle and gracious, but still the nearby musicians homed in. Was this a challenge?

"Tell you what," Big Bob said. "You take the first stanza and I'll take the second."

"Fair enough."

Sure it was fair, the musicians knew. For Bob. That way, he could assess the stranger and be first to humbly praise a good voice or the first to kindly ignore a poor one. And he got to choose the key.

They played the song once through, then Big Bob nodded at the stranger. His high tenor arced up and held for the longest time over all the other sounds.

LITTLE FLORAAAAAAAAAAAAAAAAAAAAA
HEY! LITTLE FLORAAAAAAAAAAAAAAAAAAAAAAAA
Come along, take HOLD of my hannnnnnnnnd.

People quit playing to listen. It was a perfect beginning, better than the record. Bob wouldn't take the second stanza or the third.

Someone said, "That's the purest tenor I ever heard."

"Who is that guy? Is he from Tennessee?"

When the song ended, Big Bob took off his hat and swept a deep bow. Rising back up, he said, "I been bettered."

"We'll never know, will we?" the stranger said. "Maybe singing isn't the issue."

Whoa! the group buzzed. Hot damn, man.

Nobody could reach and hold notes like that and not be on records. They knew he was a made-it man in disguise as a nobody.

Amy

The first time the tenor locked eyes with Amy, he was singing a love song with the Winterdog group, and Amy fell into
his eyes just like she did his song. He was so powerful, so
intense, like black fire. He just assumed her, in a way, as if he
knew she belonged to him the moment he wanted.

"You seeing anybody?" he asked later, when the group
was breaking up. He stood very close to her, leaning down,
and both warmth and chills infused her.

"Nobody special."

"See me. I guarantee I'll be special."

He was like a pied piper. His eyes riveted her. He didn't
blink much, but he smiled often, as if he could see much
deeper than other people and what he saw amused him. He
wasn't at all concerned about catching any kind of disease.

"I'm protected against such things," he said.

"How?"

"Faith, honey, faith."

When they made love, the animal side of him was so natural she felt exhilarated but on the brink of filth too. He was
a hairy man, front and back, and lovemaking left her with
black hairs clinging to her moist skin. The sheets, too, had to
be hand-swept. She'd never known a man to shed so much.
He stroked her back when they lay resting together, and
kissed the top of her head. Occasionally, he'd groan as if love
filled him to the hurting point.

"You're what God intended for me," he said one late afternoon, lying beside her in her bed. "I knew there was a reason for this rift in my life."

"Then maybe we should get married."

"I can't, honey, though that'd make me very happy. I got a wife, and I don't believe in divorce. What God has joined together, let no man put asunder." He kissed her. "But I love you, and I thank the Lord for giving you to me."

He seemed so matter-of-fact, just rolled out of bed and began dressing, while she lay there with this stone filling her chest. He had a wife. He had a wife. Whistling, he stood before the mirror combing his black hair. Dusty light slanted through the curtains, seeming to fall directly, and only, on him. He was that special to her.

"Why didn't you tell me?" she asked.

He came to sit by her and took both her hands in his. "Didn't matter at first, because I thought we were a one- or two-night thing. But now I recognize you for the gift you are."

She didn't want to be a gift. She didn't want to fill a rift in his life. "How can you be so religious and commit adultery? Because that's what this is, you know."

"God made me what I am. He's not going to kick up a fuss if I do my best." He studied her face. "I've hurt you, I can tell. I wouldn't do that for the world."

"Are you going back to her?"

"When she wants me. She kicks me out from time to time and I travel around if I've got any money put back."

"What if she doesn't want you? Then would you marry again?"

"Nope. I married once, for life. Can't marry again until she dies. But I tell you what, hon, if I could marry, you'd be the one. You're the sweetest little woman I've ever met."

She was his forever, no matter what. The bittersweet pain

of loving him was at least rich, full. She was living, wasn't she?

⌁

"I think he's a horse's rear," Cora told Amy. "He's working you. His deals with God are a little one-sided."
　　"He's a really good man. He'll go back if his wife wants."
　　"And where does that leave you?"
　　"I don't know. I'd marry him in a minute."
　　"He'd be the death of you, Amy."

⌁

In three months' time, he was gone. Her period didn't come and though she told herself it was the shock of losing him, she knew better. She bought an over-the-counter pregnancy test, which trivialized everything she felt. It was positive. That night she drove up toward Gates Pass, parked in a shallow pull-off before the steepest incline. She sat on a flat rock overlooking the city and played her guitar alone in the moonlight. She wanted to howl like a wild animal. She wept, but couldn't weep enough. The urge to do something, to have something, or just to be better than she was came up in her chest painfully and constantly. Oh, she didn't want to kill his baby. This she kept to herself. She scheduled the abortion, took off work for a family emergency, drove herself to the clinic and back home six hours later.

　　In her own bed, she tried to talk punishment to herself, that she deserved this, had asked for it by her lifestyle and values. But she couldn't buy that. She had loved him. Loved him still. Might love him forever. She cried off and on.

　　When she woke in the middle of the night, she padded into the kitchen for a bag of potato chips and a soda. Alone in

93

the dark, her body empty, bruised and bleeding, she thought maybe her lover had been the devil. Maybe he and God had made a deal about her. "You guys fight it out," she said, to whoever was responsible.

Every time she heard a high tenor voice on a sad song, her body grieved for a moment.

If this was how George felt, she was sorry.

Jack and Amy

Jack was by his truck in the parking lot. The Kettle was closing for the night and Amy Chandler was coming out by herself.

"Hot jam, wasn't it?" she said.

"Sure was."

"Hard to quit just because the place is closing. Want to come to my place, pick for a while?"

Jack was certain she meant to take him to bed. He wanted that to happen. This was a fine night for it, all starry cool, and he was sober because you couldn't drink at The Kettle and his afternoon beer had worn off. He drove behind her, chewing on a cigarette, thinking this was it, and wondering why he wasn't coming up already. When she turned into a residential district, he massaged himself because maybe he shouldn't even go in if he was going to make a fool of himself. He was a little reassured.

Her place was more of a sty than his. She turned on lamps and had to move plates from the coffee table and clothes from the sofa. They ended up sitting on the floor. She sat cross-legged, with the guitar over her right thigh, a posture that pulled her long skirt up to mid-shin. She didn't shave her legs, which he supposed shouldn't bother him, this being the age of natural women and men. The hair wasn't dense, but it was black, and she had a slight line of black hair above her upper lip too. Altogether, she seemed not right for his first time. His father had written about a disastrous sexual experience—Jack didn't want any such shameful failure at the outset of his adult life.

He and Amy drank beer, and he had to go to the bathroom twice, which made him feel a fool. He saw wrapped-up tampons on top of wadded toilet paper in the trash can. He didn't know if that meant she was bloody now, or what. Surely not. There should be a standard, a level of decorum. Maybe that was his father's problem. Or solution to one. He had interpreted women to their advantage.

When she switched to singing love tunes, her dark, sharp eyes shining happy at him, he tried to be bold about the whole thing and meet her eyes right on. She put her guitar down and leaned back. He could see the shade of her nipples under the blouse, wide brown smudges.

"You want to stay over?" she asked, just as simple as that.

All he had to do was say yes, but the word didn't come out.

"Better not," he said. "My dad, Lester, is coming in tomorrow."

"That's not tonight."

He didn't respond. He could see her thinking herself ugly, because his father had written about women's rough times, too, and he was sorry about what they suffered, but he couldn't do anything about it. She moved differently now, sort of crumpled in on herself, and her eyes met his only briefly.

"Next time," he said at the door, and tried to sound a little horny.

"Yeah."

He felt like an ass all the way home. His father wasn't coming in for maybe a week, a month, two months. Who knew? He cursed himself for the Texas farm hoke he was. He drove to one of the liquor stores that didn't check IDs, and picked up a carton of cigarettes and a twelve-pack. He drank two beers in the truck, just driving around empty streets.

Jack and Michael listened to "China Sundown" on the jukebox and watched two young girls pretend they could shoot pool. When one girl bent over the table next to them, Michael aped the gesture of gripping her waist, pulling her back onto himself, twisting her down and holding her there firmly.

"Sometimes I understand rape," Michael said. "You wonder what in the hell have they got to lose."

"Yeah."

"You been laid since you moved here?"

Jack thought about saying Marie, but his father wouldn't have done such a thing. "Amy offered," he said, "but you know how it goes. She's a good picker, but she's a little . . . raw."

They had become almost friends, though Jack avoided playing with Michael. Michael's songs were often dirgelike or syrupy, never driving or powerful. He was often just too heavy, like he couldn't surface to life. Jack didn't want to carry anyone. Besides, Michael sounded better alone too. That's what Jack told him. "You're a solo. You don't need Milosh or Cora or any of that group. Do your own songs."

"Thanks, buddy," Michael said. "I mean that. Sometimes I'm not sure I'm a musician at all."

"You write great lyrics, man. That's where it's at."

That was true, Jack thought. He might be wise to team up with Michael, but he couldn't entertain the idea. Even in the abstract, it had no energy. He considered doing some of the songs alone, with Michael's permission.

No. Bad idea. Michael wanted to perform. So either partner with him or leave him alone. Be straight out. No weaseling around.

⌣

A few days later, Michael came by to bum a joint, but Jack didn't keep that stuff. He rarely used it either. If he did, he'd buy it. He wasn't a freeloader.

"I'm cutting back on my medication," Michael said. "I'm tired of pushing the stone up the hill every goddamned day. I'm going to find a way to get to Mexico."

There was a spark in his eyes now, and Jack wondered if maybe Michael was crazy, truly crazy, like a modern werewolf curse, only the curse was like a full moon inside the body. He knew that wasn't clinical. He actually knew what chemical imbalances were, but the terms weren't as accurate as fiction. Lester had said that people never recognized themselves in fiction. They always picked the wrong character. That's because they didn't recognize the real pathos or grandeur of their own lives.

Jack accompanied Michael to Milosh's place. They sat in the fenced-in dirt patch of Milosh's rear yard, with grape vines straggling and struggling along a brick wall and a friendly, slobbery Doberman chewing the hell out of a tennis ball at their feet. Milosh and Michael took long drags. Jack breathed in the sweet wafting smoke and knew he'd get a light buzz just from that. The two guys talked music. They were a grassroots encyclopedia on musicians and music, but there wasn't a technical term between them. Or maybe they eschewed those and deliberately went for the common ground. No mistakes that way. A soft world.

"I'd take her back," Milosh said, and in the bright moonlight Jack could see the guy's lips tremble. His voice trembled too. "But you guys don't want to hear about that."

"That's right," Michael said. "Let it go. Get your fiddle."

"I can't play anymore. I feel like putting an armband on. I should wear it for a year."

"You're starting again," from Michael.

"I don't care. Somebody died. Me." Milosh slapped his chest.

Jack smiled a little but he didn't think Milosh was a fool. "I didn't bring my guitar," he said.

"I got one." Milosh stood up, big guy. "Guitar, mandolin, balalaika. You name it, in this house we got it."

The moon stayed slow, the Doberman slept. They played some weird songs. Milosh got up and danced in the dirt, a circle dance. "If I had a handkerchief I could do it right," he said. "If she saw me dance, I'd win her back."

"Get off that note," Jack said, and when Michael laughed so did Milosh.

"Stay off my note, damn it."

"Yeah!"

"Tune on your own time, buddy!"

"Yeah."

"Pick a song when it's your turn, not when it's mine."

They shifted music. At the early dawn Milosh offered them any sleeping place in the house and went off to bed himself. Jack and Michael went on through the warm house, across the stone front porch and the patchy weedlike grass, and climbed into Jack's truck.

"He's a good guy," Michael said. "He told me I could move in with him if I can't make my bills."

"He's okay. I don't think I could live with him."

"Yeah. There's that."

Jack felt a little slow from the beer, but he felt healthy, too, and at the start of something good. He liked both the other men well enough, but he wasn't like them. He didn't know exactly what the difference was and didn't want to examine it. It might be a trait he shouldn't have. He just wanted to be who he was without having to reshape himself because of an analytical bent.

Jack and Cora

Jack went to bed with Cora. It was a sheer accident, sort of, and he wanted to describe the cool coincidence of the whole thing to his father or someone, but that wasn't what a man did. He had gone back to her place after a party because he left his capo there. She found it for him. She was listening to an album while she straightened up the room and he just hung around awhile. He said something about not being able to dance worth shit and she offered to show him. Smoke still hung in her place and she left the front door open. They took one-two-three steps from the kitchen to the living room and on the second time through he just swung the door shut. Then he stopped trying to move and just stood slow-rocking, one, two, three. He could feel the heat rising around them, just as it was supposed to. She was a matter-of-fact woman, though, and she said, "Are we dancing or flirting?"

He said, "Both," which he thought was absolutely perfect.

He wasn't able to come and he thought maybe that was a good thing because he lasted so long. He lay beside her and rested awhile, then rose, stumbled awkwardly to the living room sofa, couldn't sleep, and went back to the bedroom. Her windows were high and moonlight crisscrossed the room and his chest. The next time he rockabyed all the way to the end and shortly afterward fell asleep.

When he woke the next morning, her place was clean, all the drapes were open, the front door was open, and the kitchen smelled like bacon. There was a plate of it crisp and still warm on the stove. He ate it all, standing there naked and in a bit of wonder at how different this day was and the rest of his life was going to be. He put on an album—she had a real good collection—slipped on his jeans and padded outside bare-chested and barefooted. She was by the side of the house, watering a pathetic patch of grass.

"My God," she said. "Get back in the house. What if someone sees you?"

He hoped they all saw him. He hoped the goddamned pope himself knew about it.

From that night, he wanted to be with her most of the time, or, more accurately, to know where she was most of the time and to be with her if he wished, only if he wished. If he felt like being at The Mill having a brew, he should be able to. The World Clock itself should accommodate the shift in his world. There was a flush of ownership and of independence, equally heavy. He laughed at himself. He was still acting like a kid. He couldn't talk about it with anyone and assumed that as he became accustomed to intimacy with a woman, the uniqueness of it would diminish and he would be calmer about the entire matter.

He preferred she not come to The Mill if he had a set there. "You distract me," he explained, and though she still came, she sat at a back table so she didn't have to walk right in front of the stage. He was being an ass, he knew, because while he wanted to own her and didn't want anybody moving in on her, he also didn't want to be paired with her publicly when he was performing. He didn't know if she had picked up on that meaning of what he said.

He told her he should just move into her little house. She lived in a bad neighborhood anyway and was usually on the edge financially. She had to "think it through," she said. "It'll probably cause more trouble than good."

He kissed her for a long moment, aware that the answer to her worry was the physical tightness of the two of them.

There was a charge between them, so powerful he wondered it wasn't visible. Maybe it was. He didn't want to be just a horny young man. He thought they had another bond. He couldn't describe it. He'd never willingly give it up.

The day he moved in, he brought his belongings loosely. One load was bedding, and the sheets and cheap blankets trailed from his arms, from the front seat of his pickup toward her tiny front yard.

Cora came out onto the porch, but stayed by the door. When he stepped up into the shade, she said, "You might as well just pee on the gate."

The word took him aback but then he realized the two of them were attuned on a higher level too, about what they were doing and why.

"I may," he said, "if the pressure gets too intense."

Jack told his dad he was involved with a woman. He eventually alluded to her age and her circumstances, how she was going back to school, broke most of the time. "She doesn't know who you are," Jack said, "or rather, who I am to you."

"She'll probably settle you down."

Jack smiled and heard it in his own voice. "I guess so."

"Treat her well."

He thought he and his dad were equally satisfied with the situation.

⌣

Someone asked Cora to give a party and Jack worked steadily all day running errands and doing small cleaning jobs. He raked the desert yard. He did it with no shirt and came in the house a few times so she'd see him. She blew him kisses but wouldn't let him near her. He liked the game of it. She had built a rough doghouse for her dog and he sat down by it and drank a couple of beers. She opened all the windows that weren't painted shut and cooked a vast pot of white beans. She baked pans of corn bread and sliced onions and tomatoes onto huge platters. She had one ice chest filled with cans and bottles of beer.

"Why so much food and so little beer?"

"People bring enough drinks."

At about 8:00 p.m. guests started arriving, some with a loaded ice chest, some with a six-pack or a bottle of wine. Many with instruments. They left the cases on the front porch or somewhere in the yard. Someone lit a fire in a metal barrel in the back. Jack ambled toward the guests near the barrel and saw Milosh rolling a joint while Michael watched. "Rule is," Milosh said, "no joints in the house, and everyone throws away his own trash."

"Who set the rule?"

"Cora. If you use her plates, you wash them too."

He didn't like her traits to be known by other men.

Groups formed everywhere. A man and woman sang a duet in Cora's bedroom, with people sitting on the bed and the sparse floor space, standing in the doorways. The couple were the reason for the party. They were songwriters and passing through from Nashville to Vegas. Jack had heard of the man, who wasn't much on the guitar but had a mellow voice. Easy and kind of tender. Jack's voice tended toward ragged. Night floated in the window and someone was even out there, looking in. In the second bedroom, ostensibly Jack's study, six or seven people shared a song with dulcimers, banjos, mandolins, and a lone guitar.

Broken heart, gold ring, needing you, good-bye good-bye. Mother's gone. Living the rest of life. Good morning, sweetheart. Where's that moon riding to?

Musicians and listeners were in the boxy living room, were outside by the washer and dryer. There had to be thirty people in the tiny house and almost that many in the yard. Cora didn't even know them all.

Good-looking young girls came too, one in a long skirt

and a half-blouse top that showed the underside curve of her breasts. Not looking at her drove Jack outside with his beer. He walked through the gate and followed the fence around the house. Some neighbors sat inside their carport and one said, "Hey." Jack nodded, said, "Hey" in return. He thought it was an important scene, one that might appear in a book he would write, or a song.

He had thought the party must be just a din of discord to all the neighbors, a cacophony. But apart as he was, sort of on the rim between two worlds, listening to all the musicians at once, he heard a different kind of music. On the grand scale, as his dad might say, harmonious. He was a little frightened as he had been as a kid, at the precariousness of the moment and his own awareness.

Cora and Jack

Cora and Jack drove to Phoenix to hear Norman Blake perform in person. The concert was in a small auditorium, the audience small, many of them musicians from Tucson and The Kettle. It was like a home gathering, especially so once she saw Norman Blake. He was like one of them, waiting on the performer instead of being the performer. He was by himself, sitting in a folding chair on a lower level of the stage, to be close to the audience. He had one microphone. He was dressed in overalls, a plain blue shirt, and heavy shoes. His hair was a little long, and he wore glasses. She felt like she was looking at him and at the same time being accompanied by him to her seat, because Jack was like another Norman Blake, only just starting out—the whole music world before him. Jack's heavy shoes were next to hers. His long curly hair outdid Blake's, and his slender, strong fingers were so obviously skilled at some art that she wanted to disappear from any presumption of companionship and be in one of the other groups. If she weren't with him, she'd just be Cora, the outsider, no expectations, few judgments. No curiosity shot her way.

But here she was. She thought of Doc Watson, one song titled "Curly Headed Baby." She had to suppress a smile at herself and her situation. She had asked for undue attention when she welcomed this boy into her life. She didn't feel shame but she thought she should. When they were seated, she whispered in Jack's ear. "I was thinking of Doc Watson's 'Curly Headed Baby.'"

He snapped a look at her, checking her mood, she knew. He got the humor, grinned and shrugged, holding the look a second or two, so it sombered, expressing now the good, demanding tension between them.

Someone in the back yelled, "Black Mountain Rag," and Blake responded in his soft, natural way, "Would you mind if I skipped it? I've played six towns in the last week and I don't want to tackle that tune right now."

"Anything at all, Mr. Blake. Whatever you want to do."

The crowd hushed.

Blake played "Lonesome Jenny" and "Ginseng Sullivan." He talked a little about his wife traveling with him. "Wish she was here."

Cora applauded with the rest of the audience, both the statement and the wife.

"Richland Avenue Rag."

"Church Street Blues."

Cora rubbed her fingertips. From so much practice on the guitar, they were calloused and grooved and rather pathetic. Some things you never got to gain. You had to learn them early, and if you missed them, you missed them. You shouldn't whine about it. Move on.

Jack leaned forward, his elbows on his knees. Now his right leg was lightly touching hers and he glanced at her. The touch was not an accident. Even in the midst of the concert he was aware of her. It was a wonderful trait.

In the middle of the audience across the aisle was Milosh. She recognized the shape of his head and that thick shock of Serbian hair. *You idiot*, she thought, of herself and of Milosh too. There was such richness in this moment though, and she wouldn't let it be sordid, not with Norman Blake's music spinning the air and everyone's heart racing beneath it. Oh. Such fragile happiness. Everyone's.

Jack and Cora

Jack was uncomfortable when Cora got intense. She could make a time be heavy and dark, like her mood was more powerful than the rest of the world. He certainly wasn't a match for it. Her sadness made her seem much older than she was. He wanted to help.

"I don't know," he said, stabbing for something to make her feel good but without lying about it, "if I love you or not. I think that's what this is."

"I didn't ask if you loved me. I'm not sure if I love you either. We're both sure, I guess, that it's not hate."

They both thought that was humorous and her sad mood lifted. He gathered that room to assert herself was a requirement of him. Better to think of it as a gift to her.

She didn't want to believe they were together only for sex. He didn't believe that was the reason. He certainly didn't believe she had a motherly role in his life. The thought was stupid and drove him up to The Mill for a hoagie.

༈

"She's good for you, I suspect," Jack's father said. They were at the DoubleTree dining room then, and Cora was in the ladies' room. "Older women are usually good for younger men."

"Yeah, probably." Jack sipped his beer. His father seldom drank, and never beer. "She likes to be in control, you know. The house neat, beds made, all that stuff."

"Most women are like that."

"I know."

"What's her history?"

"Bad marriage, two kids. She started back to school a long time ago and is about finished. She plans to leave here. Her ex-husband is a policeman." That fact, he could tell, surprised his father, maybe pleased him. "Hasn't caused any problems," Jack added.

Cora was returning. She had dressed well and seemed to fit the place well enough, but there was an edge missing. Jack wanted her to be special, not exactly sultry, though that would be better than commonplace. He would have preferred classy. She almost fit that category, but something was off. Maybe because she had been raised too poor and had too hard a life for refinement to be in her bones. She wore black slacks and a dark-green silk shirt. Her hair was up, red spun-silk knot, fine little features, a direct look. Her hands were tiny but tough. They looked as blunt and direct as she talked, *when* she talked. She was pretty silent tonight. He worried about her. He took her hand briefly and tried to look fondly at her. She withdrew her fingers and lifted her coffee cup.

He didn't have smooth ways of expressing himself. He was fond of her, damn it. Very. He'd punch anybody out who hurt her. Himself if it were possible. He'd never hurt her. He cringed at the possible untruth. Life wasn't easy.

"Jack tells me," she said to his father, "they're making a movie of your last book."

"That they are. Got some good people in it. I think it will do well."

"The others have."

"This is my favorite now. May be my favorite for all time."

"How can you write when you travel all the time?"

"I get up early and write for about two or three hours. I spend the rest of the day doing what we all do. Living."

His father and Cora were the same age. He thought perhaps

his father truly liked Cora. He thought about them in bed together, and a fiery gorge threatened him a moment. But he realized it was all in his head. He was pleased though, at the conversation between them. The slight rapport.

⌣

The next time his father was in town, Jack and Cora met him at Monetti's, an Italian restaurant in the foothills. Josie was with his father. She was dressed in silk, but it was still an Indian dress. She was going to cram her heritage down the throat of the world. Jack admired that. He too dressed like himself. He had on his ratty jeans, Red Wing boots, and two flannel shirts. His costume. His beard was quite long, the curls combed out into a thick, wiry mass, worthy, he thought, of a mountain man. While young and slender, he didn't look tame—a little wild-haired and wild-eyed. The consternation in the maître d's eyes was a pleasure.

"Could we provide the young gentleman with a jacket?" the maître d' asked.

"I'm fine as I am."

"Let's just go," Cora said, and Jack turned with her toward the door, straight-arming it open as the waiter finished his explanation about dress codes and Saturday evening business.

"Jack!" His father's voice stopped him. He motioned Cora back, but she stayed outside. Jack watched his father take charge in his lazy city-cowboy way.

"What's your best wine?"

The waiter rattled in some Romance language.

"Two bottles, please." His father gestured toward a large table on the second level, by a window. A candle flickered in a glass globe and was echoed in the window by a semicircle of flickers. "And we'd like that table."

They were led across the first level. People turned to watch them because of the brief scene at the door. Jack enjoyed that. He liked the way his father did things—no noise, no mess, no wasted time. His father had on a jacket with leather patches on the elbows, frayed cuffs, and a missing button, but the jacket had cost more than three bottles of Monetti's best wine. Things like that were stupid but they mattered in the real world. Jack could wear Red Wing boots in here not simply because his father was Lester Martin, but because Lester Martin had found ways to live in both worlds without selling his soul. Jack was going to do that too.

The waiter tried to seat Jack against the wall.

"I'll just sit here," Jack said. "Thank you kindly." He sat on the outside of the table and turned his chair so his legs and shoes were visible. He could feel the flush on his face, but he wouldn't behave as if he were flushed. "I've got to get Cora," he said, and crossed the floor with lanky steps, aware of everyone and how he must appear. But they'd be wondering why he was allowed in here looking like that. Must be somebody.

Cora was standing by the car, shivering.

"They seated us," he said. "Come on in."

"I don't want to eat there now. You couldn't pay me to put my foot in the door."

"You'll ruin their evening. Lester got us in with a bottle of wine." He chuckled. He truly felt pleased. This was a good story overall. "I'll get us a cab if you want, but I think we should go on in."

The desert sky was big and silent, black silk studded with widely spaced stars. The restaurant windows were gaudy gold muting to red, then flaming up again. Cora had worn her hair down and it splayed over the shoulders of her heavy coat like a little girl's.

"I'll feel like a fool," she said. "I storm out of there and then go back? I can't do it."

"Ignore them. You can do anything you want."

She went, but he knew her evening was ruined now and

she'd mull it over for days, making herself come up short every time. She talked as though she blamed the culture and false values, but she didn't. She made little knives to prick herself with, to whittle herself down to country-girl, aging-woman size. She was the perpetual victim. And he wouldn't be staying with her forever. He put his arm over her shoulder as they walked back in and sort of bumped into her as if he were clumsy. That always appealed to her for some reason. "I love you," he said, and felt it was true. He was sorry she hurt so much. He thought, though, that she could change her perspective and be less of a victim all the way around. She brought much of it on herself.

"Heather Russ will be joining us," his father said, and then explained to Josie and Cora that Heather was a New York model, a nice woman, an old friend. When she arrived, almost an hour later, his father watched her constantly. She was beautiful, gracious, witty. She attempted to bring Cora and Josie into the conversation, but they wouldn't join. Josie drank one margarita after the other, kept spearing bits of food and chewing them solidly with her square white teeth. She was comfortable with herself. Cora asked questions that revealed her ignorance about travel, New York, subways— common things to most of the people in his father's circle. She seemed to realize her questions weren't leading any-where except to self-exposure and fell silent. She smoked too much. When she drew on a cigarette, little lines puckered around her lips.

Carl

When the crazy skillet lady knocked on Carl's door, he had been up and dressed for only a short time.

"Could you give me a ride to the hospital?" She had a towel around her left hand.

Without hesitation, without locking the door behind him, he was beside her and guiding her toward his car. He couldn't remember her name, Dolores something or other, but she was obviously hurt—the towel had a bloody spot spreading. "You hold that hand up," he said. "And bend your elbow more."

She obeyed him. He opened the car door for her and kind of ushered her in. She made sure her skirt didn't get caught in the door, and that amused him, her calm femininity even now. Women had ways like that, automatic, live or die, but do it right. He scooted into the driver's seat. The sun already streaked the sky a dark pink, but the temperature was pleasantly cool. He felt a strange mixture of the familiar and new, the way he used to feel traveling to a fair or to meet a buddy coming in on a train. Something happening.

He gunned the motor and drove toward the street. "Which way?"

"Left. It's the county hospital I have to go to, down on St. Mary's Road."

"South Tucson?"

"Just off the freeway."

She didn't seem at all afraid or nervous. "You hurt real bad?"

"It's going to take some stitches." She unwrapped the towel a little. He couldn't see the wound.

"What happened?"

"I was cutting some frozen meat and the knife just slipped off and jabbed me in the hand. A frozen ham. I was going to cook a slice for breakfast."

Carl grunted. "Could've microwaved it a little."

"I don't have one. I don't trust them."

He didn't believe her, though she sounded convincing enough, very matter-of-fact. He suspected she had tried to cut her wrists and then got scared.

"Let me see that wound."

"It's okay." She hummed for a moment or two, then said, "Microwaves scare me. Seems like I can feel them inside me, the waves. They have to go somewhere." She hummed again, then ceased. Carl felt her looking at him. "You haven't answered me," she said.

"I didn't hear a question."

"Where do the electromagnetic waves go?"

Was this craziness? Maybe not. "They fade away, I suppose, if nothing gets in their way. Get weaker and weaker till they die out."

"What if they don't die out?"

"I don't know. I probably don't want to know either."

"Maybe they don't." She nodded her head emphatically as if they had settled the matter to her satisfaction.

She went back to humming and he was glad she did. He was wary about the line of conversation. From a sane person it might be okay, but there was no telling what she'd do for or because of those waves.

At the emergency room he stayed nearby while the nurse removed the towel. The cut was lengthwise, which surprised him—he had expected a self-inflicted crosswise slash—a call for attention. But this was a genuine wound, still streaming a thin line of bright red. "You come on back, Dolores," the nurse said. "I'll get you ready for the doctor."

The injured woman glanced at Carl. "You don't have to wait for me. I can walk back."

"Sure," he said. "I'd let you do that." He stalked over to the tiny waiting area and picked up a magazine. He wasn't going to read it but she'd know he planned to wait. When she was out of sight, he found a pay phone and called Dave Stone at home. "I won't be in this morning," he said. Stone argued. "I got personal business to attend to," Carl said and then hung up. Then he stepped outside for a cigarette.

An hour and a half later, which Carl thought far too long for a simple repair job, they were back in his car. "We could stop somewhere for breakfast," he said. "Been quite a morning for you."

"I'd rather go home. I could fix you some ham and eggs. I'd like to."

"Nope. You keep that hand inactive for a while. If they didn't tell you that, they should have."

She was a placid little thing, sitting with ankles crossed. She had on white socks, folded down, and penny loafers. Her fingernails were cut short, even and clean. Looked like another no-nonsense woman, but he knew better. He remembered those skillets in his yard, and it seemed like she left calling cards at hospitals on a regular basis. The nurse, after all, had known her name.

He ended up doing what she wanted, going to her house. The upholstered furniture and drapes were dull shades of brown, but rag rugs added ovals of woven red, yellow, blue, and green before the sink and by two chairs. Her coffee table had a lace doily in the center and a low, round bowl filled with yellow silk flowers. A golden-brown afghan was rumpled at one end of the sofa and she folded it and put it over the back. "I sometimes fall asleep here," she explained. Her small home reminded him of the easygoing neatness of his own background. Commonsense living, no needless spit and polish and perfection.

Temporarily one-handed, she fried ham, fried the eggs in a separate skillet, and fixed milk gravy from the meat drippings. She put an orange on the table by him. "You could peel this," she said, "and put the segments on a saucer for us." She served them both on white plates patterned with wheat sheaves and loaded the table with saucers full of other choices: bread, butter, apple butter, strawberry and apricot jellies.

"Looks like I come off best in this transaction," he said.

She was one of the plainest women he'd had any dealings with. Her face was narrow, with a receding chin and a prominent nose, so she had an ugly profile. Her teeth were all right, white and even, but they were too small for her mouth. When she grinned, the edges of her upper gum showed. Her eyes, though, they were fine. Real direct. Huge. Brown and moist, with that dreamy look that might mean she was nearsighted. Or, maybe, on medication. She had a cute nose.

He was no great looker himself, he considered. So he could come down from his high horse.

When he left her comfortable little place he passed Callie's and was ready to doff his hat or even go in for a minute if she asked. He thought he saw a shadow behind the lace curtains, but since it didn't materialize into Callie, he went on home.

⌁

At Sam's Steak Place that night, Callie sat with Mel's wife, ordered her free dinner, and asked for a tune from Carl, "Crapshooter's Rag." She liked knowing the names of tunes. He left the stage three times, to two-step her around the floor. She was a graceful dancer and certainly a woman a man didn't have to be ashamed to squire around. But she seemed too big for his arms, a cumbersome burden. Carl couldn't explain the sensation, since she wasn't a large woman and followed his lead precisely.

Callie was unusually quiet on the drive back into town, but Carl didn't pry. A woman's hesitation was worth noting—overall they were pretty sensitive, and if they planned something unpleasant, they avoided talking about it until they were asked. She'd open up soon enough. He used the time to grumble about Mel's penchant for singing mostly in C. "He's got a real narrow range, you see, and wants to pitch the song for his best sound."

"What do you expect him to do, Carl? Give up singing and let you guys play instrumentals all the time?"

"A few more instrumentals wouldn't hurt." She was looking out her window as though the conversation were just an aside. "He could also," Carl added, "pass a vocal on to another member of the band once in a while—Dexter does harmony now. He could do lead. I think he wants to. He sings when we're packing up. Or Mel could maybe invite guests now and then. Give some less fortunates a chance to show what they can do. Maybe some of the young musicians."

"It's his show, isn't it?"

"Yes, indeed," Carl said, and fell silent. The waters had gotten deeper. The creek was rising. He felt selfish and petty and needful of apologizing to Mel and maybe to Callie.

When he parked the car Callie put her hand on his forearm. "I'm sorry, Carl. None of that was called for."

"Well, I'm sure glad to hear it. Thought I might have to shoot myself."

She rewarded him with a genuine sweet laugh. "Could we have coffee at your place this time?"

At first that surprised him, but once inside he realized she wanted to reassure herself that he was the only resident. She carried her coat to his bedroom and, he imagined, checked out the bathroom.

When she returned, joining him in the kitchen, she said, "I saw you and Dolores this morning. I guess you took her to the hospital."

"Yep. Somebody had to."

"What happened?"

He told her.

"I wonder why she came to you?"

"Oh, I'm up early on Saturdays. I imagine most of the renters around here know that."

"I'm up early too." She took the cup he offered, turned toward the living room. "And I've told her to let me know if she needs anything."

"Have you now?"

"Yes." She sat in the center of the sofa, indicating, he assumed, that he was to sit next to her. He complied. Callie clicked the television remote through a bunch of silent channels, stopping at the weather report. "She picked you for the same reason I did, I suspect. You're a good man."

Her left hand rested on his thigh. "I don't know why she picked me," he said. "And I'd just as soon not discuss it."

"You mean it's not my business?"

Now he felt rude and ungrateful. Callie wasn't a petty woman. "I mean it's not mine. Feel a little dishonest talking about her." He took the remote from her. "You want to watch something?"

"No." Her lower lip was slightly indrawn, held by perfectly white teeth. "You meant that, didn't you? That it's her business, not ours."

"Yeah. I don't want it to be mine."

She nodded. "Neither do I."

Carl, leaning forward, continued skimming channels. Callie ran her hand down his back casually, ending the stroke in a light pat, the hand remaining where it was. He knew what he was supposed to do now—kiss her, kiss again, let nature take them on a nice ride. "That feels good," he said. "Wish I wasn't so tired." He faced her. "Maybe you'll forgive me this time?" He hoped she'd take her part like a lady, and she did.

"You do like me, don't you, Carl? I mean, if you don't, I'll stop coming around. You don't owe me anything."

If he wanted out, now was the time. "Couldn't want anyone better than you," he said, "young or old." It was true, but didn't answer her question, not if she gave it a little thought.

He insisted on walking her the short distance to her house, and there she kissed him, three light kisses, one on each corner of his lips and one in the center, the kind of kisses that were gentle and inviting and that he'd always liked. Her scent was like a flower powder and he liked that too. This was the warm affection he valued and longed for, but it wasn't enough for him to be a man with her. "Good night," he said, feeling a little foolish. "Maybe I'll have another chance and won't be so tired."

"I'll see to that," she said.

When he got home, he fondled himself a little. Dead as kingdom come. He turned out the lights so she'd think he'd gone to bed, and he listened to the radio in the dark.

∾

A week later, two-stepping with Callie at Sam's, he knew she had romantic notions again. She was not a quitter. She wore a red silky dress cut square down from her shoulders, so the white fullness of her breasts was partly visible. Her shoes were tiny strap contraptions, but she had no trouble moving smoothly and quickly. He didn't have any liquor at all, but drank some strong coffee. It couldn't hurt. When he drove them home, she sat close to him, hand on his thigh. He tried concentrating on his lower parts to rouse what he might. Above the whole desert, the moon floated cool, white, and distant, and he felt that way himself.

At her doorstep, she said, "You are coming in, aren't you?"

"You bet. Been thinking about it all evening."

He kissed her a lot just inside the door, and let his breathing get heavier. She took his hand and led him toward the bedroom. "I'd best use the bathroom first," he said. In there, he manipulated himself so he wasn't totally flaccid, then went in the bedroom. She had undressed.

"You look even better without your clothes," he said. "I wouldn't have believed that possible."

He removed his boots and she helped him finish undressing. It was pleasant, except that he knew he would fail. "Hope I'm man enough for you," he said.

He made love to her mostly with his hands, though he was able to rise enough to enter her for a few seconds before going soft again.

"Happens sometimes," he said. "Thought it might not tonight, with a lady like you."

"Don't worry about it. We'll get better as we get more comfortable with each other."

When he got a cigarette and sat on the edge of the bed to smoke, she opened the bedroom window. Then she lay behind him and lightly caressed his back. He had to ask her for an ashtray and she went in the other room, returning with a saucer. That made him almost mad but he didn't say anything. The least she could do was let him smoke in comfort.

"Why don't you sleep here tonight?" she asked.

"Better not. No telling what kind of sexy thing you'd do to me in my sleep."

She watched him dress like she was fond of him. Even got up to button his shirt. She was still naked. A bit more modesty, he thought, wouldn't hurt her. Then he regretted his attitude. He was judging her harshly because he disliked himself at the moment. He couldn't blame women for expecting him to be what he was supposed to be. They were sort of trusting themselves to him.

"You're a fine-looking woman."

"I'm glad you think so. I try to take care of myself."

"Done a damned good job."

She put on a robe to walk him to the front door. He kissed her once more, nuzzled her neck, and made a soft grunting sound. "Hope you had a good time," he said.

"I did. Hope you did too."

"Me? Just looking at you is enough for me."

"We'll see about that."

He hated himself all the short way home. He'd gotten himself into a fine predicament, having to perform what he couldn't perform, having to get better at what he couldn't even do in the first place. He looked toward Dolores's house. Maybe there was a high sign about him, invisible except to women: THIS MAN CAN'T SAY NO.

When he tried to sleep, he kept seeing his wife, that dark-haired beauty, hearing the clipped, hateful voice she could use. He'd loved her. A person couldn't choose who to love. He dreamed about a woman who was both his wife and Elizabeth and whose forearms dripped blood. He was supposed to drink the liquid or he'd die, but he wouldn't. He woke in a shudder, with a cottony mouth, and stumbled into the kitchen for a drink. Too unsettled to go back to bed, he put on a tape of him, Amy, and Cora. The dark got filled with nice company and gradually he calmed and fell asleep on the sofa.

✌

Carl steeled himself. Somebody's ego was going to suffer, hers or his. Seated together inside Callie's house, with the next move hovering like an unspoken command, he took her hand. "I got to be honest with you. There isn't anything wrong with you. Nothing at all. But I'm not much in the manhood department. Don't know why it is and can't do a damned thing about it. You're going to get disappointed over and over. I'm good for squiring a woman around but not much else."

She surprised him. "Sex isn't everything, Carl. My husband had problems as he got older. We can manage that. We're fond of each other, we get along. I like your music and your easy ways. And if you really want to do something about your problem, you probably can. Doctors can help, I know. But only if you want it. I just like you, and I want you to like me."

"I do."

"You think about it. Meanwhile," she stood up, "no sex until you say so. I'm going to get us some coffee and we'll watch the weather or news." When she brought the coffee, hers was in a cup with saucer, his in a mug. She had bought an ashtray, too, and she put it on the coffee table in front of them.

"I do appreciate the ashtray," he said, and gratefully pulled out his cigarettes. "I was wondering, Callie, what you do during the day. Thought maybe you were into bridge clubs or something like that."

"I sometimes play bridge. I also paint, and now—since meeting you—practice the fiddle. I'm in a senior exercise group at the community center. We walk twice a week and swim once."

"You paint people? Landscapes?" He grinned. "Houses?"

"These pictures are all mine."

He got up, studied the one on the opposite wall. She joined him. "I like soft colors," she said.

"I can see that."

She took him into a back bedroom where many canvases leaned against the walls. Two paintings in progress were on easels. "I'm trying to capture the desert now," she said.

She had a good sky going in each, one like dawn, the other

like sunset, and the desert surface was pretty fair, scattered with hardy, harsh browns that were occasionally transformed by a bit of delicate blossom, yellow, red, purple. But the cacti were flat. Not strong, or distorted, or ancient. Tamed into green that hadn't weathered anything and couldn't withstand much. They looked as if they had alighted there temporarily instead of coming out of the ground and holding on forever. He felt fonder of her. She tried.

They watched the weather forecast across the country and drank tepid coffee.

"I want you to think about something, Carl."

"I do that most of the time. Especially around you."

"I'm serious. I want you to think about us living together. It doesn't have to be right away. In fact, we could just spend more and more time with each other, you know, test the waters. If we keep getting along like we do now, we could pool our resources and cut down on our expenses. A lot of senior citizens are doing it. It makes sense for people our age."

He was flabbergasted, but he covered his reaction. "A young thing like you?"

"We respect each other. We're active people, in good health. We have hobbies. As far as I can tell, we don't have any habits that'd get in each other's way."

She was serious, obviously. "I got some drop-by people, you know," he said.

"But you wouldn't lose them. I like music. You know that. It's one of the nicest things about you. And I'm trying to be a part of that."

She didn't urge him to stay. She kissed him real sweet at the door. "Please think about what I said."

"Can't help it. Haven't had a better offer." He walked back to his place. He felt crowded and hot, like his collar had gone two sizes down. She moved way too fast. And the music was his. Nobody'd ever pushed against that before.

He remembered back to her arguments for Mel's running the show. She had a good view of the situation. Actually, Carl admired Mel's business acumen. The musician had maintained the gig at the steak house for nine years before Carl joined, and had done so without having any blood or social ties to the owner. Mel was just good at keeping a band together, keeping the music pleasant and danceable. Maybe it was sort of boring and predictable, but they did add new tunes fairly often. Someone in the dinner-and-dance crowd would request a song or one of the musicians would pick up a new one, and the band would add it to their repertoire. "Lyin' Eyes," "Could I Have This Dance," "Tulsa Time." Vocals dominated. Steel guitar and fiddle wove. Carl had maybe fifty songs he'd like to add, but it wasn't his band, or his gig. And it was his pleasure to play well whatever they chose. When he was asked, he suggested an old favorite or a new one he'd picked up from the radio. Most of the time, he just played fill, or took a break, and those were easy enough to do. To be highlighted, well, that was rare. He stayed prepared with his signature songs. He wished he'd never breathed any hint of dissatisfaction, especially to Callie. He didn't want to add that tone to his place in the music world. Mel was good to him and the band was good for him. Sometimes, a man had to breathe a little discontent, but he should do so while solitary.

⌣

Carl unfolded the note he'd found under his windshield. The writing was scrawled and wavery, like the hand holding the pen had been trembling. The language and charge of the note appalled him. He glanced sharply toward Dolores's cottage. The craziness was on her again. He had a choice of getting to work on time or checking on Dolores. He headed toward her place and hesitated when he saw the front and side windows. He might need some help. Each pane was a scene in vivid colors, the dominant one red. Jesus on the cross, Jesus praying, a knife through a heart, another through an eye.

He knocked harshly. "Dolores?" He knocked again, then just turned the doorknob and walked in.

The woman standing a few feet away wasn't the Dolores he knew. She was wearing layers of clothing: jeans on the bottom, shorts on top of those; a man's shirt beneath a leather vest; a dish towel hanging from a belt around her hips; a red-bead necklace, draped like a tiara, crossing her forehead. Her face was animated, intelligent, superior. And a little frightening.

"I don't need you," she said. "I've got everything under control now."

"Sure you do. That's why you wrote me that nice note about me and Callie."

"Miss Bitch." She pretended to spit at her feet.

Carl didn't know what to do with her. "You don't want to talk that way. It isn't like you."

"It isn't? Fancy that." She spun toward the kitchen and he followed warily. For all he knew, she could come out with a knife. She was turning on the faucet, scrubbing her hands. At first he thought their vivid flush was reflection from the painted window, but then he realized the skin was raw.

"Dolores," he said softly. "Let me help you."

She dried her hands on the dish towel hanging from the belt, leaving small smears of red. "I can see right through you, mister. You and everyone else. I know what you got planned, but you won't get me. I've packed my belongings and I can leave," she snapped her fingers, "just like that."

This he couldn't handle. He was too old. "Could we just ride down to the hospital?"

She ran from the room, into the bathroom, but he was right behind her and got his foot in the door. He forced

127

himself in and grabbed her shoulders, but she twisted free and climbed in the bathtub.

He was panting. He lowered the commode seat and sat down. "You're going to kill me," he said. "I can't pick you up and carry you there."

"Get out, get out, get out, get out," she said, louder each time.

"I'd like to," he interrupted gently. "But I think you know as well as I do that I can't. If I have to call the hospital, I will."

She sat down, too, and he could see how very weary she was. Gone was the soft brown of her eyes; they burned.

"No one really likes you," she said. "You give out minutes like pennies."

"Very likely, you're right. That's all I got to give." He lit a cigarette and waited.

When a quarter hour had passed without her speaking or trying anything, he said, "Well, are you ready for a decision? I can call the hospital or we can take a ride together."

She wouldn't look at him, but in a moment she pushed herself up. He offered his hand to help her from the tub. She ignored it, got out by herself. He guided her toward the front door without touching her, as if only to catch her should she fall.

He drove slowly, chatting about the traffic, the weather. Her hands, resting on her legs, were trembling. He imagined her whole being was.

At the emergency room, before they took her into the examining room, she said, "Carl," and the voice sounded lucid, like Dolores.

"Yes."

No response.

"Okay," he said. "Accepted."

❧

Carl briefly considered going to the Emporium. He called instead. "I have to take a sick day," he said to Dave Stone.

"You don't get sick days. No pay, that is."

"I know. But this is a courtesy call and my reason for missing a day's work is sickness." He hung up, and settled the gorge rising in him. He thought maybe getting fired would be the best thing. Taking charge and quitting at the right moment could be better. But the upside, as always, was he had a place to go every day, a real job he could do better than competently, and a paycheck.

He lay down on his bed, setting the alarm for a thirty-minute nap. When he woke, feeling a little rested, he got scrapers and turpentine from his tool cabinet and went back to Dolores's. Midafternoon, he heard the front door open and close.

"Carl? Are you in here?"

Callie wanted to help, but Carl shooed her away. He knew enough about women to understand that Dolores would be driven mad in another way if she ever learned Callie had been privy to this dishevelment.

Carl checked out library books on manic-depression.

"Bipolar disorder," he said aloud in his small living room. "Like top of the world, bottom of the world."

⌣

Dolores, home again, needed a ride to a therapy session and Carl drove her on his lunch hour. Michael Halloran was there, softer and paler than Carl had yet seen him, slouched in one of the orange plastic chairs. He was holding an unlit cigarette. He nodded at Carl, then, noticing Dolores, drew himself more erect. "Hello," he said, with true familiarity. Of course they knew each other, Carl realized. They had visited some of the same places in many ways.

Carl wondered if all manic-depressive people had the same shape—receding chin, pointed nose, rounded shoulders and back. Michael was curving in on himself and that's what Dolores looked like when she was coming out of her high period, like everything good and strong in her had been pulled out and left her body no straightness at all. It would sink down and down. What they had was an ugly disorder—he wouldn't call it a disease anymore—and a permanent one. Those people had no hope of ever being okay. They had a battle for life.

⌣

"Dolores needs some friends," he told Callie, "and some outlet. Anybody'd go crazy just being in a house all the time."

Callie, who had taken it upon herself to clean his kitchen-counter tile, continued shaking scouring powder. "People can't help someone who won't help themselves," she said. "Dolores has probably run through all her friends."

"She just goes off her medicine."

"That can get old. Even crazy people have a choice. She chooses the mania instead of following a prescribed diet and taking her medication as directed. So she's choosing, in some ways, at least, to put pressure on her friends."

He watched her scrub the caulking with a toothbrush. "Maybe we should invite her to join us one Friday," he said. "Give her some music and good companionship." He saw how well that went over, though Callie didn't speak right away. She appeared engrossed in one particularly recalcitrant tile.

"You might take her alone," Callie said. "She would be more relaxed, I'm certain. No woman, you know, enjoys being a tagalong."

She had a vengeance against the countertop. He understood why. His own way, when he got around to it, would

130

have been to pour bleach on the tiles a few times. Simpler. But woman art included ways of cleaning. Let her shine.

She put the cleaning items away shortly, both of them aware of her discomfort and his inability to address it. "Shall we skip this Friday?" she said, standing with one hand on the screen doorframe.

He pretended to consider the question, then said, "Just this once, maybe. If you don't mind."

"I mind and you know it." She let the screen door bounce shut. He watched her stride off, anger evident in the long steps and the swish of skirt around her calves. Even angry, she was in good style. White hair a uniform purity, coiffed in place. That was a hardy woman, for sure.

⌣

"Sometimes I can," Dolores said. "But not tonight."

They were standing at the edge of the dance floor, near the band's table. "Sure you can. It's just a two-step, like this." Staying in the confined space they held, Carl demonstrated smoothly, twice, the only dance moves engrained in his body, two slide steps to the right forward, slight pause shift, two slide steps to the left forward. With a little different rhythm, the steps would work for most dances.

She almost smiled.

"Now put your hand in mine," he said, holding up his left hand and lowering his right to her waist.

She moved out of his reach. "No."

He felt foolish but he stayed there, and in a few seconds she came closer again, her head down. He could take steps with her, but no glide. No real dancing. She felt heavy to him, and he was sure she felt even heavier to herself. Her body was too slow and pliable, as a sleepy child's might be. Other dancers slipped by them, some able to whirl as they did so, some going in that wide, straight-ahead gradual loop that

131

was the simplest and oldest way. She looked up and around and he took the opportunity to wink at her. "Doing fine."

They kept on till Mel and the others ended the tune.

Carl escorted her back to the band's table.

"I'm sorry," she said, and as he seated her added, "Sometimes I'm alive."

He chuckled. "I believe I've seen that."

She was very plain, he decided, more than he had thought before. A little brown wren. Can't make a silk purse out of a sow's ear, he told himself, and then argued with his judgment. Beauty is as beauty does. She can't help what she's got. She had tried to please him despite her discomfort. Sweet inclination. He didn't know where or how he had obtained his high standard for female comeliness. It might be to make up for his own shortness.

She wanted Tuesday evenings to be hers, just the one night a week. She knitted while he watched television or worked at some chore.

He never knew what she was thinking, but he wasn't anxious about it. Odd, how a crazy person could seem trustworthy. Maybe because blame had no place in the equation. It was outside the two of them, faced in tandem.

⌣

Carl and Dolores were in his living room. It was about 10:30 p.m. and he had just watched the weather for Oklahoma and the rest of the states. Dolores stood up and began unbuttoning her dress.

"You got something new in mind?" Carl asked.

"I want us to go to bed together."

"Do I have any say?"

She stopped. Her lips twisted a little, not a pretty sight.

"Not," Carl said, "that it's a bad idea."

She resumed undressing. She didn't remove her underwear.

She wore full white panties, and her belly rounded out a little. She had heavy breasts held tight in cups sewn like cones. Pointy, which he found unnatural. He felt sorry for women in that regard.

"That garment doesn't look too comfortable," he said.

"You don't think of me as a woman," she responded, heading for the bedroom. "But I'm not just a sick person, you know. I was a nurse and a mother and wife. I'm more than pills and hospitals."

"You off your medicine again?"

He was in the doorway to his bedroom and she was on the bed. Her plumpness was sort of attractive, healthy and firm.

"Nope. I just want us to get intimate here and stop talking all the time. You're always checking what I'm thinking. I don't tell you everything I think."

He undressed to his shorts and undershirt and lay down beside her. "I've got about thirty years on you," he said, "and I worked today."

"We don't have to make love. I just want to get intimate."

She tugged his right hand so he lifted his arm and let her snuggle up against him. She lay real still then. He could feel the stiffness of the bra against his skin.

"That contraption complicates things somewhat," he said.

She didn't answer. She breathed easily. She wasn't actually rushing anything and he was grateful. She touched his jaw with her fingers, her forearm resting easily on him. He was aware of his own older body, particularly his stomach.

"That's my investment," he said. "Other folks got a big bank account. I got a bellyful of good food."

"You're a good man," she said, and lay still. In a little while, she undid her bra and lay back down. Her breasts swelled against his side and he liked that. When he realized she might be falling asleep, he turned completely on his side and scooted down so he could press his face against those fine, soft breasts. She placed her hand on the back of his head.

133

He wondered where women got that kind of knowledge, a gentle way of doing the right thing. He wondered why they didn't all have it. He started to remember his wife's contempt and shied away from it quickly. He breathed in this little crazy woman. She was apparently asleep. He eased toward it too.

During the night he covered them both up. She didn't snore or even toss. She slept like she had a clean conscience no matter what was roiling in that mind.

"You always see Callie on Saturdays, right?" she said the next morning. "And sometimes Friday?"

"That's the way it's fallen into place."

"Then maybe I could see you on Sunday afternoons? Tuesday nights and Sunday afternoons."

"Why do we have to plan it?"

"Forget it."

"I don't know what you want with an old dude like me," he said. "But if I'm home those days, you're welcome. Someone might come by to play a little. I wouldn't want to turn them away."

"I like music." A few minutes later she said, "It soothes the savage breast."

"What?"

"Music does."

He was amused by that and knew she referred to something he should probably know about. She wasn't savage. He understood that she was talking about a wild heart.

She wasn't the least bit interested in learning to fiddle and she didn't pull the intimacy bit again. She just came over. Amy dropped by when Dolores was there the first Sunday, and Dolores read a book. Her foot tapped, though, and occasionally her eyes would indicate she was listening to the music and not reading words. She didn't have a jealous bone in her body, he thought. If she weren't crazy, she'd be okay, better than okay.

She sang a few lines now and then, from old, common

tunes, not loudly enough to be calling attention to herself. More like recalling the words or drawing on a sweet feeling. Songs like "Believe Me, If All Those Endearing Young Charms." Maybe she knew all the words. Her voice wasn't forceful and had a natural tremble. It made a kind of pleasant background. Touching. Her eyes were sometimes filled with gentleness and he thought it was terribly unfair that she had to be saddled with an imbalance that jerked her away from herself and threw her into collision with the world.

❧

Kettle Musicians
Old Time Fiddlers Association Benefit Concert
for Paula Welker

Saturday, October 14, 8:00 a.m. till the music stops

Bring sustenance, shade, seating, and MUSIC
Stage Provided
Take Road 112 just before the Desert Museum Turnoff
DON'T TOUCH THE SAGUAROS!

Guest performers include Hector Porter, the Glenn Brothers, Pete and Molly's Cajun Do, Lass Grass and Cabin Fever (two all-girl bands), the Old Geezers, Big Bob, Shady Grove, George Dey and Susan Harfield, Winterdog, and . . . . YOU!!!!

Fall sun still hot with a steady droning glare but a soft breeze ground level, sometimes whining around the saguaros; rough stage with massive tarp tied to poles, sweltering shade, a few straggly mesquites dangling pods; trucks and campers with tarps fashioning rectangles of shade that moved with the sun; dirt filtering up from dancing feet; beer in kegs, paper cups crunched near trash bins, tin foil over tamales, someone grilling hot dogs and hamburger meat, potato salad shared; red sweaty smiling faces, slippery hands.

❧

Harmony rushing through the valley.

If the ocean was whiskey . . .
SHEEEEEEEE'SSSSS MY LITTTTTTTTT EL . . .
Just because I said I love you, doesn't mean I really do . . .
Wish I had pretty Della Mae to miss me when I'm gone . . .
Way back in the hills . . .
We don't have Blue Ridge or Lee Highway but we're where
   you'll spend some better days . . .
Grab that gal with the red dress on, spin her once, walk her
   home . . .

Waltzing in desert moonlight, small-group music wafting up like good night.

One car at a time, trailing up the narrow road to and through Gates Pass, headlights tiny, tiny, cresting over and there below, the city valley, studded with streetlights on velvet black.

❧

Kettle Brew Newsletter

Don't forget square dances at the YWCA on Fifth Street, second and fourth Saturdays of every month. Volunteer musicians needed (especially a bassist).

Dan Brennan's Irish penny whistle group will play at house concert December 10. For details, call Lona Craig 892-4435 and look for announcement in next newsletter.

Amy Chandler's Lass Grass took third at the new band contest in Flagstaff. CONGRATULATIONS, GALS!

Open mics:
Pete's Bar and Grill, 7205 Broadway, Thursday evenings.

Dusty Inn, 1432 South Wilshire, Wednesdays, 10 to midnight.

Health Sandwiches, 42 South Fourth, Saturday and Sunday, 2–6.

Anyone who knows the lyrics to "Snow Deer" or "Candelabra Polka" please call Shirley Bates, 891-8814.

"I know," Amy told Cora, "that this won't last forever. I may even have to leave Tucson someday. Sometimes I know I want to leave, that I've got to do something else. But this is magic, isn't it? This whole troop of people. This whole country."

"You're part of the magic," Cora said.

"You too."

"No. I do love it though."

"Then you're part of it." Amy reached out and squeezed Cora's knee. "Wherever you go."

Carl

Carl saw a slender, rather short man sauntering down the aisle, backdropped by light from the front. His features weren't distinguishable, but Carl recognized the set of shoulders. Billy Wilcox. Carl wanted to scurry out the gate at the end of his counter, but he held his peace, even contained his smile, and just stretched out his hand at the appropriate moment. "Took you long enough," he said. "Thought you'd dropped me off your route."

"You're the one who moved."

"A good point."

Billy was coming around to the gate, but Carl said, "We don't need to stay here. Just give me a few minutes to clean up and we'll find a place to eat and talk." He went to the restroom, scrubbed his hands, and, removing his hat, rinsed his face and combed back his thin hair. He rolled his shirtsleeves down and buttoned them. Back at his station, he donned his jacket and headed for the fiddle section, where Billy obviously was. Billy still looked like a kid. Fair face, bony, no extra fat on him, no wrinkles, pleasant half smile and blue eyes. He had had a brother who looked about the same but got into some bad habits and died young.

"Get a fiddle, Carl," Billy said. "Come on. Let's do one right here."

Carl didn't want to because Billy was his friend and he didn't really feel like sharing that with Dave Stone. However. He took down a fiddle he'd played before, quickly tuned it, and as soon as it hit his shoulder, Billy took off into "Lady's Fancy."

Like new air. Like handshakes. Like a good meal. Like a good cry. A yell. A stomp. When it ended, he felt a bit of shadow in the atmosphere and knew Dave Stone was behind him. He lowered his fiddle but heard "Do another," and it wasn't from Billy.

They did two more. They stirred up the dust of the place. They were paying for Carl's early lunch break.

Carl introduced Billy to Stone. "He plays with Prairie Sons."

"You mind if I get a picture or two?" Stone said over a handshake.

"No, I'd be flattered," from Billy.

When Stone returned, Carl and Billy posed, fiddles down on opposite sides like part of the frame.

Stone said, "Thanks."

"I don't know that Dave Stone," Carl said, when they were outside. "Seems like a decent sort today."

◡⋰

They had lunch at the café where Carl was always treated well and where he knew the waitresses by name and knew the best meals on the menu.

"It's hard to believe you're in Tucson," Billy said. "I'll be able to picture you here now. You ought to come to Branson. I mean, if you can move, move where they'll treat you right. You're a better fiddler than I am. You could do studio work easy. I'd find a place for you. I know some people."

"I think I'll stay here."

"I'm serious, Carl."

"I am too. I had one move in me, and I took it late."

Billy laughed. It was infectious. He was a nice man, Carl thought. He had always been so. "I play with a pretty good group here. It's about all I want to handle."

"Am I going to meet them?"

"If you want. We don't practice much. If we do, we meet at Mel's. It's his band, his gig."

"You're the one I want to play with," Billy said. "So it's up to you. I've been trying to work up a good version of 'Turkey Tracks.' You know that one, don't you?"

"I got a version."

Carl decided to take the afternoon off. When he told Stone, the man nodded toward Billy, only a little bit of quarrel in his expression. Carl and Billy spent the afternoon in Carl's living room, playing, listening, catching up. Carl taped their playing and made a copy for Billy. Billy went through the stack of cassettes. "You have some company, I see. Amy. Cora. Michael. Gary and Shirley. Jack. Dennis. H."

"There's more musicians in this town than tornadoes in Oklahoma."

Later, they drove out to the steak house for a full dinner. The Flying Texans didn't play weeknights, but Carl believed in giving the steak house business every now and then, and he wanted Billy to see the place. It wasn't shabby.

"They serve about two hundred dinners each Friday and Saturday night," Carl said. "Steady dance crowd too."

"Next time, I'll visit on a weekend."

"You do that. We'll highlight you."

"We'll twin-fiddle them to death."

"I should warn you Mel isn't much for sharing."

"Oh. Gotcha. I've run into that at times. Everyone does. Part of the business."

There was the empty stage and the two of them sitting at a table, willing and able to warm up the place. But—it wasn't their stage and it might not be fair to Mel. Carl didn't know what Billy thought about it.

Billy slept on his sofa. Carl lay awake for a while, thinking about what he had passed up years ago. He wondered where his ex-wife was, and then was glad he didn't know. He thought he'd forgotten what she looked like, and then a memory would unfold like a photograph and he'd see her pert face and delicate hands and how she looked when she listened to music or turned to survey the crowd. He felt the memory, always tinged with derision. He turned off that thought like he'd turn off a spigot.

He was glad Billy had stayed married and stayed, maybe, content. That long-ago swap was a different kind of investment, and a good one. He thought of trying to move to Branson and put himself up against—or just with—other fiddlers, young and old, ambitious or lazy or whatever. He didn't want that kind of life. Maybe he never had wanted it. Maybe he hadn't sacrificed at all. He could hear Billy snoring lightly. A good sound. A friend sleeping under his roof. He lapsed into wondering where Billy would be if he, Carl, had taken off with the band that day. He coughed, grunted at his wayward mind. Thinking backward contorted the heart and spirit. Choked up the chest. He hadn't asked if Billy had heard anything about Elizabeth or Webb Tucker. Now he considered what it meant that Billy hadn't brought them up. He sighed and it seemed to him the sigh turned deeper, into a moan.

He gave up on sleeping, and thus it overtook him.

◡

Carl sat at his desk to open his mail. He sliced open each envelope, stacked them, and saved the one from the Oklahoma Fiddlers Association for last. When he finally picked it up again, he turned it over, then held it to the light, and finally slipped out and unfolded the sheet. They wondered if he would serve as one of the judges for the state fiddling championship. Webb Tucker of Tulsa and Phillip Worthington of Dallas had agreed to serve. Webb Tucker. The man Elizabeth had taken up with on Carl's ten thousand. Carl laid the letter aside and lit a cigarette. Would he be a fool if he went or if he didn't go? Maybe *coward* was the more accurate word.

Elizabeth might as well be sitting in the room with him, head tilted, eyes bright and waiting. He felt uncomfortable. He cleared his throat a few times. He refolded the invitation, tucked it partly under the leather binding of the desk pad. For the next few minutes, he leafed through the junk mail, made certain it was all headed for the trash, stacked it neatly anyhow, and left the room without reading the invitation again. He wasn't likely to forget it. He wasn't likely to accept it either.

Done is done.

Callie came over to ride with him out to the steak place. She had acquired a new dancing outfit, a red skirt with a white ruffle, a white blouse, and red shoes with very low heels. More substantive than usual. She was taking country swing lessons at the senior citizens center. He remembered the letter off and on all evening, little rushes of a compliment on paper.

Callie wanted to teach him country swing.

"I like the two-step," she said. "Don't get me wrong. But you're a good dancer, Carl, and you'd pick up country swing in no time. We could add a few turns and variations to what you already do. We could also pick up a line dance or two."

"Musicians can't dance," he said. "One of God's rules."

She grimaced. "Don't give me one of your adages. You just don't want to learn."

"Some things you should be afraid of learning."

"Dancing?"

"Then all the gals would be after me."

That gave her thought, but she still wanted him to learn. "We could practice Sunday afternoons," she said, "when you're free."

"You can swing with Dexter," he said. "I keep Sundays open for playing music."

"Yes, I know," she said.

He didn't answer the slight accusation in her tone, since

they both knew Dolores did not play. Dolores was, however, in his mind, a boon to the playing, part of tuning the room itself.

Dexter, the steel guitarist, had taken to dancing with Callie once each Saturday night. He was a widower and didn't eat much and didn't smoke. He was a steady musician, uninspired but totally reliable, and he didn't outshine Mel. "Dexter's got less weight to carry and is right graceful."

"I want to dance with *you*, Carl," she said later. She was sitting next to him on his sofa. On the screen, the weatherman said it was raining in the Midwest, and tornados were dancing all over. "But I'll dance with Dexter if he's the only one available."

On Sunday morning, Carl sat down by his phone, lit a cigarette, and called some buddies in Oklahoma to talk over the contest. The first two didn't know anything about Webb and Elizabeth, but the third, the most gossip-prone male Carl knew, said, "Yep. Tight as corn on the cob. They had a little row and he moved out, went with some other woman for a while, then went back to Elizabeth."

Carl wrote a neat little message to the Fiddlers Association. "I'd be proud to serve as judge." He signed it Carl W. Bradshaw, Esquire, because that's how he learned to sign when he was a boy and he thought it looked better than just a plain name.

He had the event ahead of him now, with all its possibilities. He controlled it, let himself think of it in dollops. Even conjecturing the weather was a pleasant part of wondering.

SET III

Jack and Cora

Well, Jack thought, he certainly knew more about women now. A man was supposed to second-guess them and way in advance.

"Why," Cora said, "would you do that? Fix chili for you and Michael and not for me?"

"There were only two cans and Michael said he was hungry. You didn't say anything."

"I shouldn't have to. When I cook for me, I cook for you too."

That sounded right when she said it, but it *felt* wrong. Jack was indignant but without the words for defense.

⤙

Jack had only thirty minutes' notice that Cora's daughters were coming to visit.

"It's not going to be easy on me either," she said. "At least it'll be done. They know about you. They want to see you. It's understandable."

"Is it understandable that I don't want to be here? I wouldn't mind bumping into them somewhere or meeting them with warning, but this is uncomfortable." He looked toward the bedroom they shared. "Everything is pretty obvious."

"If we hurry, we have enough time to make a false impression."

That amused his worry away. He moved close to her somberly, as he had discovered she liked, and began unbuttoning her blouse while he watched her eyes. He loved the shift of emotions his touch could bring. He had wondered if any other woman would react the same to him. Even now, with the imminent threat of her children seeing him, she gave in to his touch. He saw it, felt it in her skin. "Love you," he said, then tore himself away. He grabbed his book and harmonica from his side of her bed, jerked the wrinkled spread neat and flat, as she usually did. In the spare bedroom, he sat on the bed, propped the pillow up and leaned against it, and laid the book facedown near the edge of the bed.

She was busy too. He could see her washing the ashtray, and from faint outside sounds knew she had opened the front door and the front double window. Sun fell across the desert willow tree and cast shadows into the house.

Her daughters were his age. One exactly, and one two years younger. They were in college. He could have been in a class with them. Maybe he would know them by sight.

He wondered if they were anything like her.

"I'm putting on some music," he said. He started an album and as the needle lowered, went into the bathroom. He tried to force a comb through his hair, gave up, and tied the long curls low, at the nape of his neck. He combed his beard a little, brushed his teeth. He tucked in his shirt, plaid, wrinkled, missing a button, then hurriedly took it off, threw it in the back of his closet, and put on a solid white one, also a little wrinkled, but very clean. He had on sandals and thought about shifting to Red Wing shoes, but decided the sandals had an older, more conservative look, arty maybe, something daughters might like.

He goddamned would like a beer. Two or three of them.

When they came, he expected a knock, but instead heard a voice so like Cora's it confused him for a couple of seconds.

"Hello? Hello? We're here."

Cora came from the kitchen, beaming, but with a pink flush on her cheeks, and he stayed by his bedroom door. The face owning the "Hello" was very pretty, quizzical, and a little shy, as if saying, "Did we interrupt anything?" That girl was blonde. Her eyebrows were so pale the outer ends were invisible. "Hello, Jack," she said. "I'm Mary." She raised a delicate hand to the girl who entered and stood behind her. "And this is Leslie." That one had dark curly hair, cut short, and large, strikingly blue eyes. Both were pretty. Neither looked like Cora.

"Pleased to meet you," he said. "I'm Jack Martin."

"We know," the dark-haired one said. "Nice to meet you too."

Since awkward was the norm, they were all on equal footing, or something like that. The girls sat on the sofa, before the open window, and he and Cora took the chairs, separate. He felt on display and was aware of his entire body. He could feel his toenails, which he had—he was glad—clipped the day before.

"Could I get you some coffee?" he asked. "Or a soda?" He took a risk. "A beer?"

"Nothing," the blonde said. "Thanks though."

"I'd like a Coke," the other one said. "I'd ask for beer, but my mother might have a hissy."

He got up quickly, aware from a glance that she was teasing him and her mother.

"A beer it is," he said, and hoped to God Cora didn't contradict him. She didn't.

After they'd talked through the pleasantries that allowed them to be comfortable and were nearing either touchy subjects or boring evasions, he said, "I'm going to leave you alone for a while, and walk up toward campus."

"You don't need to leave, Jack," Cora said. "We're fine."

"Really," Mary said. "Please stay."

"I'll stay next time," he said, with a little bow to each of them. It felt stiff but right. "You don't see each other often. You probably have things to talk about."

Then he was outside, the sun so freshly bright and the

air like it was from another country. They were nice-looking girls. He took long steps, then slowed down, felt a deep nostalgia as if something sad had happened and he was remembering it before it had completely occurred. He thought of his mother and all the times he hadn't seen her. He thought he might cry and he was too damned adult for that. He tried to pick up his pace, couldn't. He eventually came to The Mill, having in some ways walked across the fields behind his and his dad's ranch house, having sat on the porch with the house empty, while a steady but easy wind blew through the front door and side windows.

᠅

"For you," Cora said, and handed Jack the phone. He thought it'd be his father or mother, but it was a soft, vaguely familiar female voice.

"Know who this is?"

"No, can't say that I do." He saw Cora glance at him from the kitchen.

"Marie."

"Marie who?" Then he realized—the Marie he'd driven madly to her Colorado home that one bleak winter. "How the hell are you?"

"Really good. I'm in Boulder now. I got married but it didn't last long. Shouldn't have done it."

Jack smoked five cigarettes while they talked. Somehow an ashtray appeared beside him. Then a cup of coffee. He was almost embarrassed at the sheer pleasure he felt from this girl calling him like that, out of the blue.

"Any chance of you coming up this way?" she said, when they were winding down, and he thought of Cora then.

"Maybe," he said. "Not real soon. I'm living with a woman." He knew that was the wrong way to say that, but he couldn't think of any other options. "Cora. Her name's Cora."

"Tell her hi for me. She there?"

"Yeah. She's in the kitchen."

"Let me speak with her."

He wasn't sure about that. "Better not," he said, and felt a pleasant conspiracy between them. It was the most private he'd felt in a long time.

"I was just going to tell her to hang on to you. You're the best man I've run into."

"Hope that doesn't stay true," he said. "You deserve even better." He was so goddamned glad he'd said something good that he missed her response.

When he said good-bye and hung up the phone he felt the silence in the house. Cora came into the room. "So who was that?"

"Girl named Marie. Friend of mine."

"Why haven't you mentioned her?"

"Never thought about it."

"You ask me all these questions about my past, then you don't tell me about yours."

"Didn't know I had one till now."

Cora laughed then, and he knew he was onto something. He was finding the right way to talk to women. He had just stumbled onto it.

ᴗ̣

Cora told Jack he didn't have to dress up for her friend's wedding so he didn't. It wasn't a fancy wedding, anyhow, just a kind of foolish one. The woman was maybe forty-five, but she was all cinched in and bosomy, in a white leather skirt and top, white fringed boots. She was marrying a guy a lot younger than her, but Jack liked him okay. He was a quiet man, almost bald, and seemed amused by the whole setup. The woman had written their vows and had copies printed for the friends standing around. They were at the old desert mission, in the courtyard, though a lay preacher was performing the ceremony. The mountains beyond were a deep blue, like a Zane Grey setting, and an occasional desert breeze fluttered the saguaro blossoms. Jack liked the larger setting, but he thought the wedding was gaudy in spite of their downscaling. The mission, though, was fine. Fine. Had history behind it, Spanish and Indian. Dirt floors in some of the smaller structures. Painted statues. Tohono O'odham. Navajo. Yaqui. Jack liked this part of the country, the mix of it all. So did Lester. Lester liked so many things, people, places. Jack didn't know what roused the deepest passion in his father. If he was ever lonely, he hid it. Maybe he wrote it out.

Jack leaned down to whisper to Cora. "You want to get married?"

She was surprised and very pleased. He had behaved well again.

"No," she said. "But I'm glad you asked."

"I mean it," he said later that afternoon.

"I know. But you're not old enough to know what it really means. Besides, I don't want to be married to a younger man."

"So what are we doing?"

"Waiting it out."

He liked the lightness of Cora's touch. He liked her singing. She said her mother had a beautiful voice and sang lots of ballads and church songs. Her mother had worked in a factory. A petite red-haired woman. A very good mother.

⌣

Late summer, Milosh rapped on the screen door and Jack saw he had his fiddle case with him, and Michael trailing along behind.

"We're going up to the Red Dog bar. They said we could do a set. You and Cora should come along. The four of us will knock them dead."

Jack wanted to go and he didn't want to. He wanted to perform almost anytime, but he wanted it to be good, quality. He wasn't sure they could all come together impromptu.

Cora had come up behind him.

"Will you come, Cora?" the Serb asked, and she looked at Jack, which Jack appreciated. He already understood his approval wasn't necessary.

"Sure."

They didn't have a sound system with them and there were only five people in the audience to start with. Jack didn't try to outshine his friends. He just played well and a little quietly. When he looked up, someone listening would nod at him or raise a glass and he'd nod back.

Michael sang one of his own songs, "In Our Back Alley." The lyrics were good, and the rhythm rolling, but the tone was still somber. A downer. Maybe Michael was meant to be a recluse. He could go deeper into whatever drew him.

On his next turn, Michael sang "Summer Wages" and Jack felt the familiar flush of jealousy and anger, but it eased quickly. He wasn't really jealous. It was just being male. Only the one line got to him, about stealing a woman. It was overt flirting with Cora and a dare to Jack. Its main effect was to prompt the question *Why was Cora out singing in a bar with three young men anyhow?*

He disliked himself for asking the question. No. He disliked, rather, what he believed was the answer. Cora liked young men. What did that say about him?

Alone with her later, he said, "Would you sleep with Michael if I weren't around?"

"Are you leaving?"

"That doesn't answer the question."

"I don't know why you would ask it otherwise."

"You slept with Milosh and with me."

She was sitting on the bed but leaning down, pulling blue slippers onto her feet. "Oh," she said, and sat up. "You want a list of how many men I've slept with? Including boys? Let's see. There was David—my husband—and Milosh." She looked at him without anger. In fact, she seemed loving. "And you."

"Okay," he said. "Just don't ever sleep with Michael."

He realized a couple of hours later, when he was on the front steps in the slow twilight of the desert, hearing the murmur of voices in this rich, mixed, voluble neighborhood, that he had in effect told her someday he'd be leaving. He wasn't sure about that. He could marry her. His dad might give him a caveat or two but he'd support it. He tried to visualize himself driving down the road with Cora in the front seat of his truck, and then to visualize himself in this house with her for, say, one year, two, five. He couldn't get past the moment. But he could see the stock of his favorite rifle, his granny's old Chevy, the books lining the ranch house walls. He could see only one thing at a time. That's who he was. He saw Cora in a dark room, on a bed, nude, pale and lithe, turning over and rising, heard her lulling voice. He got up and went inside.

✧

He thought of Marie sometimes, about getting in his red truck and just showing up in Boulder. He had her number memorized and he'd written it down on the back of a music-store card. Marie was like a song he couldn't remember the words to.

✧

Jack answered the knock at the front door. It took him a moment to recognize the couple, acquaintances from The Mill.

"You said we should stop by some night," the woman said, and the two of them came on in. Cora appeared from the back room where she'd been typing. The young couple were surprised by her, Jack knew. He saw the surreptitious looks. He made introductions, went to the refrigerator for beer.

He was uncomfortable with the situation, but what the hell, he hadn't known they'd actually drop by.

"You remind me of someone," the young woman said, looking at Cora. "Some actress." She wouldn't let it go. "God, it's on the tip of my tongue." She hummed a melody.

They chatted about The Mill crowd, about the guy who had been in a motorcycle accident years ago and now spit obscenities every other breath, about Bill the harmonica player, who wasn't really very good, but was entertaining.

"He talks too much," Jack said. "If you got to explain what you're doing, you're not doing it very well."

The young woman kept staring at Cora. "I wish I could remember." She hummed the song again. "That's the theme song. If I can just get it . . ."

"*The Graduate*," her boyfriend said. "That's the theme from *The Graduate*."

"Yeah, that's it," the girl said. "You remind me of what's-her-name. Mrs. Robinson."

Jack was tickled in spite of himself. The stupidity of the girl and the goddamned accidental accuracy and symbolism of the thing. "Mike Nichols," he said.

"What Mike Nichols?"

"He directed it. *The Graduate*." Jack raised his beer, looking quickly at Cora. She was amused. He was glad. Their relationship had some sophistication. "Great music," Jack said. "Great music."

˜

Jack put a wide board behind the front seat of the pickup so Cora's dog could go along on the trip to Texas. They zoomed down the highway, under wide-open skies with white trailing clouds, watched the landscape shift from desert to rolling hills, rocky crags, flatland. He punched the radio on sometimes, sometimes put in tapes, and sometimes just let the wind roar through a cracked window.

Cora was scared about the whole thing and he was, too, but he wasn't going to let her know that.

"Just be yourself," he said. "They'll like you."

"I wouldn't like it if you were my son and you brought someone my age home."

"Don't think that way."

"Better me than someone else. Shows I've at least not lost my common sense."

They arrived at the ranch house two days before Christmas. It was dark, snow piled up against the porch. He had to clump around in the backyard checking the propane tank, had to bring in wood and start a fire. The place looked pitiful for a famous man's house, but he enjoyed the rarity of it all.

"We don't lock the doors when we're gone," he said. "Hunters sometimes stop in to clean their kill or just warm up a bit."

He boiled some coffee in a white enamel pan and found a bag with a little sugar for her. It was hard but he pounded it to powder with a knife handle.

"We always roughed it, I guess," he said. "Didn't think about it. Lester's not here much anymore."

All their talk seemed phony and disconnected, like old family members getting together after a long separation, but Cora wasn't family and they hadn't been apart one night since he moved in with her. She wasn't herself though. She was this quiet, withdrawn, timid, and angry woman. He sort of understood it. She kept petting her dog. He understood that too.

He took the cushions off the sofa and put them in front of the fireplace. The turquoise material looked warm and inviting. Such a simple thing, yet he felt he'd turned a little magic in the room for her. He was the provider. He stretched out on the pillows. "Come over here," he said.

"No."

"Okay." He rolled to his other side and watched the flames.

A few minutes later she asked, "Your dad'll be here tomorrow?"

"Or the next day. You can't tell with Lester."

"Which room's ours?"

He got up and showed her. It was his old room. He had been a kid in this room and that made her seem wrong for him. "The heater's going," he said, "but it won't warm the whole house up for a few more hours."

She showered and came running into the living room, shivering and dressed in a gray sweat suit. She hunkered down next to the fire. "God was that bathroom cold."

They made love on the cushions and the utter starkness of that was arousing. His house, no curtains, dead of a Texas winter, his father and Josie on the way. He knew Cora hadn't climaxed and he understood why. The whole thing was really goddamned sad.

In town the next day, his grandmother and aunts bought little gifts for Cora, a makeup bag, potholders, some earrings. Josie gave Cora a framed photograph of a church on the Laguna Pueblo reservation in New Mexico. Lester gave her copies of his novels. He'd written pleasant, gracious notes inside the covers. Cora did well. But she did look older now, and tired. At night she curled up next to him like a freezing bag of bones that might scatter. He felt he'd suddenly grown up, like he'd ridden into manhood somewhere between Arizona and Texas. He went hunting on Christmas Day, got eight quail and cleaned them in the backyard. He cooked them up too. He wasn't just music and words.

The Kettle Crew

Kettle winter nights: an iron stove popping wood heat in one corner. People entered shivering but grinning. Wet guitar cases. Susan now played fiddle with Winterdog. The band had sent a demo tape to Disney and had an audition in three weeks. If they were chosen, they'd go to Japan, play in that Disneyland. Some of The Kettle's own were moving on, up with the big boys.

"God, I'm jealous. I'd give my eyeteeth . . ."

"Proves it can happen. All a group has to do is be good and stick together. No backstabbing."

Milosh played Winterdog's demo on *The Blues Show*, *The Gospel Show*, and *The Bluegrass Show*.

"That ain't gospel, man," a listener called to complain.

"*My* gospel, Mr. Telephone Caller," Milosh said. "Friends are the good word the world round."

༝

The Kettle Sound

"Homegrown Tomatoes," "Big Sandy," "The House of Blue
Lights," "Blue Railroad Train," "Slow Train Through
Georgia," "Blues for Dixie," "Thirty Days," "Take the A
Train," "Blue Eyed Boston Boy," "Gulf Coast Blues,"
"Memphis Woman," "Angel From Montgomery,"
"Hurricane."
"SALLY GOODIN."
"Cotton-Eyed Joe."
"Whiskey Before Breakfast."
"Draggin' the Bow."
"UNCLE PEN." BASS WALK WALK WALK—hear it
SINNNNNNNNNNG!
Monsoon summers.
Rain slicing up afternoons, dance peppering flooded streets.
Jam sessions with all the windows open, rare wet desert air.
Desert blooms, sudden and wild.
YELLOWREDYELLOWPOPPYGREENREDPOPPYGREEN.

Carl and Cora

Carl hurried from Sam's Steak Place as soon as the equipment was locked away. He sped down the worn blacktop and through late-night streets to downtown. The Kettle hadn't yet wound up. He took his fiddle inside, dropped a five-dollar bill into the can, then thought better of leaving that temptation and took it back.

He went to the kitchen door. "I'd like to leave my donation in here," he said. "Make sure it gets where it's supposed to."

A young girl washing dishes said, "Just leave it on the counter. I'll tell Pam. She's doing the door tonight."

"She isn't there."

"She will be. If she's gone on home, I'll see to it."

Carl went into the back room. Gary Hargrove had a sofa to himself, Shirley at the moment seated on the sofa arm, wives and a new guy—a Dobro player—in folding chairs forming a loose half circle. Seated on the floor and leaning against the sofa, no guitar in hand, was Amy. She was intent on the dobroist. As the tune faded, and the bottleneck whine outlasted the other notes, she said, "Hey, that was really nice," and looked totally sincere. Her eyes were shining at him. Even when she saw Carl beckoning, and gradually gathered herself up, her eyes darted to the Dobro guy.

"Pop," she said. "Good to see you. Break out that fiddle."

"Got a proposition for you," he said.

"Just what I like. Propositions." She sounded sprightly, as always, but she was dividing her attention.

Carl got right to it. "I'm going up to Oklahoma on the

161

seventeenth, judge the state fiddle contest. I'd like to be accompanied by a good-looking gal. I'd pay everything and give you two hundred dollars to boot."

"You wouldn't have to pay me, Pop."

"Wouldn't let you go otherwise. Be some fine jamming too. And you could back me up for the dance. It's likely to be filmed for the state association. You'd spruce up their history."

She was tugging at her hair. He sensed a "No" on the way and didn't want it. Such a small thing he was counting on. He should've asked sooner. Yesterday, even.

"I don't think I'd better. I've missed a lot of work lately with my back going out and they're sort of watching me. What about Susan? She can do backup. Winterdog's not leaving for Japan for two months, and they're all short of cash."

"Susan's a fiddler first. It might be a slight to ask her. Besides, I'd rather you went. You wouldn't have to be there on Friday. You could come up later, even Saturday afternoon would do. I'd rather we went up together, but I'd rather have you for those two hours than anybody else the whole time."

She was torn, he knew. She didn't want to disappoint him. Again, her dark eyes shifted toward the skinny young man holding the Dobro. Carl knew he'd lost. He didn't really begrudge her. It was the way of things. But he felt this twinge, like a foreboding that he shouldn't have agreed to judge.

"Ask Susan," Amy said. "If she can't, ask Cora."

The object of her affection was attempting a break on "Have I Told You Lately That I Love You."

"You like Dobros, I see," Carl said.

She laughed, a little softer than usual. "I didn't know until now," she said, her fondness shining for him, too, as if they were conspirators in her budding affection for the Dobro guy. "You could ask Cora first, Pop. She could use a nice break right now."

Amy was gone, smitten, maybe out of his life in the natural course of the world. Carl eyed the prospective beau closely. Worn jeans, too large but barely long enough for his lanky frame, wheat-colored hair thick and cut ragged. A poor guy. The almost-hillbilly appearance could be deceptive. Shy, maybe, but not humble. Perceptive. If he was kind, Lord knows he'd be a better match for her than what she had settled for before.

This time, Carl thought, he'd had poor timing. Selfish coot that he was. He had waited too long to ask Amy to accompany him. If he had asked her earlier and locked her in, she'd be right with him. She wasn't a will-o'-the-wisp with her word. She might *lie*, but that wasn't the same as going back on her word. She wouldn't do it.

He didn't have to take anyone with him. Skilled seconds were always at contests. He'd run into someone he knew. He just didn't want to show up alone, like he lived that way every day. He wanted a little proof of his being all right.

For looks and music, Susan would be fine. Excellent musician, better than the men she played with. Real pert, lively little wire. But *too* wired most of the time. And he didn't really *know* her. Carl looked around for Cora, but she and Jack weren't there. He joined Gary Hargrove and Shirley Bates, playing a faint harmony line behind the tunes. Anything more would rattle fragile Shirley into silence.

Carl called Cora Saturday afternoon.

"I want to help you out," Cora said, "but I'm not as good a backup as Amy. You sure she won't go?"

"She's locked her sights on another musician. We won't be seeing much of her for a while."

"I'd have to get some Valium from someone," she said. "I hate to take it, but I know I can't get on a plane otherwise."

"I'll get you liquored up," he said, "and you won't need nothing but caution with me."

"I'll go if you can't get someone else. Susan maybe. Or how about Paul's guitarist?"

"Prefer a good-looking gal like yourself."

"Okay. Only if no one else will go."

Women were always doing that. Being helpful if there was a gap but not committing till they were sure.

"Don't want nobody else," he said.

◡⋰

Carl tried not to think of Elizabeth being at the Oklahoma contest, but she wouldn't go away. When he got in bed at night, his old body needing rest and sleep, he tossed, playing possible scenes of meeting her. Surely she wouldn't go, wouldn't risk encountering him. But he wanted her to be there. Wanted her contrite and shamed, pulling him away to explain and ask pardon. He'd do it—forgive her. All it'd take was a little recognition that she'd done him wrong. He wanted her so obviously fond of him and indebted to him that people who knew them would understand he'd behaved like a gentlemen, not a fool. He tried to conjure up a pleading, sorrowful Elizabeth asking him to move back to Oklahoma. But he could only create two Elizabeths, the flushed and bright one who took the envelope of money, and the one he encountered a few times after, with a veil behind the eyes. What was the veiled Elizabeth like? What had that woman really thought of him? If he followed the conjecture he would be critiquing himself and never know the truth anyhow. He considered instead what he really wanted. Was it to have her back? Her orchid face came up and he shook his head. He couldn't handle her when he had her. He wanted her to be regretful, to value him more, maybe above the self-loving Webb Tucker. Yes, above Webb. Equal to, at least. He wanted the chance to say something final and important, something that would make him not only generous but wise: "Don't worry about the money, Elizabeth. If I was worried about getting it back, I wouldn't have given it to you." "No, I don't think I'll move back to Oklahoma. I'm pretty satisfied where I am." He suspected she might know it wasn't true.

He could fall asleep only by thinking of the final night of the contest, when the judges performed. Since he was the senior judge, he'd be last. Elizabeth would be in the front row, watching. Cora would wear a long dark skirt, a pink cotton blouse, and have her red silk hair down. He'd be in black. He'd ease into a Texas swing tune, then tear the place apart with a hoedown. Then, for his final tune, he'd play "Sweet Molly's Waltz." He'd turn toward Cora for that one, and play like he was making love to her with music. People would get so quiet; the notes would woo them all. Later they'd talk about Carl and his new woman. He always had a pretty one. How did the old goat do that? He could fall asleep to the memory strains of the waltz. It was the loveliest waltz of the hundreds he knew.

∴

"Why don't you want me with you, Carl?" Callie asked.

"Won't be nothing for you to do. I'll be in a judge's booth all day Friday, looking up friends and jamming that night, then in the booth all day Saturday and have to perform Saturday night. Think I'd take a woman like you just to leave her sitting around for other fellows?"

"I could learn something."

"That's what I'm trying to prevent."

"I mean I could learn the fiddle a little better."

"Oh. Then how about I show you some more tricks when I get back."

"I understand what you're saying, Carl. You don't need to be evasive. If you don't want me along, I don't want to be along."

He felt rightly chastised, sorry for her, and ashamed of himself.

"I'd feel responsible for you, Callie. I'd want you to be with people who would welcome you and help you enjoy the music. You're a gracious woman. You're not accustomed to being taken to an event and then left alone. At least I don't think so. I'd be worried about you all the time. Not a jealous worry. A social worry."

"I like festivals and people. I can occupy myself. But I don't want to go now. I'd be worried about *you* all the time, that I was hampering your style."

She didn't leave his place right away, and he supposed that meant she wasn't as mad as he thought. She had sort of won the argument, after all. She had called it as it really was. While it was true that he would have worried about her comfort, he didn't want to worry about more than Elizabeth. That would take all of his wherewithal. And, ugly truth that it was, he didn't want Elizabeth to see him with a woman like Callie. Callie was a decent woman, and attractive. But he was seeing her through Elizabeth's eyes—old, no competition, a companion to provide good food and dull talk. He'd make up for the slight to Callie. He shook his head in aggravation. Who was he kidding? It wasn't possible to make up for something like that, especially when he'd done it knowingly. Leaving her behind when she wanted to come along. He didn't know what he was doing with Callie. If she said she was through with him, he'd take a deep breath and sigh with relief. So why didn't he just tell her they were no good together?

Because she was the kind of woman he should want. He should be honored that she chose him. He'd once heard a man say, "Any woman who'd have me, I wouldn't have." Maybe he shared the sentiment. Then, again, maybe he just didn't have any initiative. Spine.

⌣

Dolores just said, "I'll miss our Sunday afternoon."

"I'll be back by late Sunday, but I'll be useless company. I'll have to sleep and let the music run out of me. Won't be able to talk or listen. But, tell you what—I'll bring you a bonnet or something."

She laughed and said "bonnet" every now and then for the next hour. That made him laugh too. He wouldn't have to make anything up to her. The little crazy thing didn't want much. A fun word was enough. *Bonnet.*

⌣

"All you have to do," Carl said to Cora, "is stand by the steps up to the stage. When the young contestants come down, give each of them one of these silver dollars."

"Do people know you do this?"

"Not if I can help it. If anyone pries, say you represent the Fiddlers Association."

"But I don't."

"You're representing me. That makes it no more'n a quarter inch from the truth."

He'd decided to shake Webb Tucker's hand if he was put in that position when the judges met. He could greet the man as a fiddler, give him his due. The opportunity didn't arise.

The pole-tall, black-eyed man with a wide-gash mouth and a husky voice didn't offer his hand. He just said, "Mr. Bradshaw" without even a nod. Carl responded in kind. "Mr. Tucker." Carl didn't look around the crowd right then, though he was sorely drawn to. He didn't want to see Elizabeth and weaken his concentration. And he wanted to be *ready* to see her, preferably with Cora in arm.

From 9:00 to 11:00 a.m. he was wearing headphones and sitting in a vented but windowless wooden booth, which in his opinion was much like an upgraded outhouse. He kept his tie and hat on even when the booth felt like a broiler, because a man judged better if he felt and looked like a judge. He listened closely. There were only three in the Junior-Juniors, sweet little scratchers, but nine in the Juniors. He thought he could pretty well guess the age of the kids, maybe even the gender, by the sureness of the bowing. But times were changing, and he could be mistaken. A couple of the fiddlers he thought he knew. The Jennings boy, who would be fifteen by now, his mother backing him up. She had a Texas-style backup that any player would envy. He thought another one might be Walter Tilley, a red-haired, sloppy fiddler who had so much fun playing that a viewing audience would be crazy about him. Dancing to his music, though, might be a chore. His timing was creative. Carl discounted any hint of identity and rated only the traits of the music. He hoped a girl won, but in this arena he wouldn't give one a boost. Fairness all the way. When he finally stepped outside with his score sheets, he almost ran into Tucker.

"Good lot, wasn't it?" Tucker said.

"Pretty fine."

"Which Junior'd you like best?"

"Number five."

"Me too. Let's see what Phil's got."

He didn't watch the people's faces as the judges' results for that category were announced, but his gaze roamed over the crowd in general. He caught a quick wave from the Jennings boy's father, Lou, and waved back, saw Darrel Morehouse, probably here with the Belshes—they followed contests and festivals in the Midwest, had favorites they supported. They couldn't dance or sing as far as he knew. They just liked to listen. They ate a lot, and thus had a pretty solid presence on Earth. He thought for a minute of Callie's possible impression of them, of this whole shindig, and, feeling that he should apologize even at this distance, shuddered. She hadn't done anything wrong, he reminded himself. He was listening to his own opinion.

Just then, off guard for one second, he saw Elizabeth

moving through the crowd toward the judges' booth, and he felt foolishly and dangerously weak, as if his heart couldn't provide the oxygen he needed. His mouth went dry. Elizabeth did stand out. White, white skin among all these weathered folks, a thin gold necklace sliding against a scarlet silk blouse. He forced himself to look away.

"Carl!"

He tried to look surprised, but he didn't speak. He touched his hat brim automatically, and regretted that courteous gesture. He should've waited to hear what she had to say.

"Carl Bradshaw." She took his arm and leaned into him like he was going to squire her around. She smelled sweet and clean, and her hair against his cheek made him long to cup her head to him. Only that. A comfort. "I was looking for you," she said.

"Well, you found me pretty easy."

"I dressed up just on the chance I'd get to see you. Glad I did too. You're handsomer than ever. That Tucson climate must agree with you."

"Yep. Does that." He pulled his arm free to reach for a cigarette and compose himself. He'd expected something different, something grander, maybe just good. He squinted at her. "What you been doing with yourself, Elizabeth?"

"Trying to make a go of a restaurant. I opened it three months ago and have had a few setbacks." She brushed at his lapel. "You know how it goes. The best of plans."

"No. Don't make many plans myself." Then, without being able to stop himself, he said, "Did plan on hearing from you long before this."

There was the veil.

"I know. I'm ashamed of myself, Carl, but I haven't been able to get any big sum together. I didn't want to pay you in dribbles. And you never said when I had to pay you back. Not that I remember."

She was so lovely, he had to force himself to look away

before he believed her just from longing to. He glanced at the announcer. "'Bout time for me to go back in my little cubicle here." He couldn't yet let it go. "Didn't think I had to say when, Elizabeth. Wasn't thinking in terms of years though."

"You didn't tell me that. You needing money?"

"Nope." He had to counter her. "Never have."

"Come on, Carl. Don't make me feel bad about something I couldn't do and you never asked for. I didn't even ask you for that money. I didn't even know where you went to."

"Wasn't that you just commented on the Tucson climate?"

"I learned that last week."

He grunted. Her big, luminous eyes had set a little harder. "I got some judging to do," he said. He crunched the cigarette under his heel and returned to the booth. He was winded and hot. And empty. He was sickened with himself more than with her. He should have risen above her and he hadn't. He hadn't said anything to erase the bad between them. He was still wanting a woman to fill up his ego when he wasn't man enough to even have one.

⌣

Twenty-eight more contestants in the first round, age groups 20–40, 40–60, and old-timers 60+. Windswept Oklahoma hill. Mic-roaring music and wind, occasional bursts of applause, *yahoos* and *whoooooops* before the sound man could shut down the judges' line.

Difficulty: 1–10
Tone: 1–10
Danceability: 1–10

Coffee break, tallying marks. Elizabeth. Women and old age. Stifling heat. Fairness. Attentiveness. Smoke-burned throat. Elizabeth.

Carl bought himself and Cora steak dinners, carried them

on double paper plates to the wooden tables under the nearest pavilion. "You want to go listen to the new bands, jam a little, or go back to the room to freshen up?"

"Freshen up. Maybe jam a little later."

"What's that feller of yours doing this weekend?"

"Fishing."

"Young men still do that?"

"He does. Hunts, fishes."

"Everything but work."

She ripped a biscuit in two, dipped a corner of one piece in gravy, and bit it off neatly. After swallowing, she said, "He doesn't have to. The family's got money coming out their ears."

"Don't stop a man from working."

She liked that. She laughed. He liked it himself.

"He's very young, you know," she said bluntly, meeting his eyes. "He was raised by his dad in the midst of a big family. He doesn't know what he wants yet."

He nodded his understanding. The situation was awkward for her.

They walked the campground after the sun had set and the air cooled a bit. He passed a very brief time with the Jenningses, since their boy would be fiddling tomorrow and he couldn't give the appearance of favoritism. He settled in longer a couple of places, with some good Oklahoma people who were interested in him, which wasn't the same as nosiness. Seeing them now, he realized how much he had missed them. They were part of his past, of Oklahoma. He had struck out as if he were a young man off to sail around the world and had taken an old man's short ride to Tucson. Starting over with only a little left to finish. He mentioned some of his new friends, Tucson folks. Thus, if they ever encountered each other, his Oklahoma and Tucson communities, the link was made. Sometimes the only connection in people's lives was music, like a country they had all visited and remembered, as much a part of a place as the seasons. There were people in his past he remembered through the instrument associated with them. An old guy about Carl's age now, Baynard Wilson, who had played a gourd fiddle. That's what Baynard had started on and he always kept one around. Made them for other people too. There was a Johnny Appleseed in the nation's history, and a Gourd Fiddler in Oklahoma history, private history. Experiences. Past. Some shared and some unshareable.

Each time he and Cora walked on or each time a person approached where they stood, he was looking for Elizabeth and scared of finding her again. He'd never be ready for her. He still wanted to make the perfect statement to frame a moment for the two of them. One he could look at without flinching.

The smells of cooking and cigarette smoke wafted everywhere. And music. Strains of different songs mingled, altered when another musician entered. Constantly changing. So it would go most of the night, the blend like a separate melody altogether. God, he loved music and musicians. When he stood still and closed his eyes, he'd swear the universe was playing strings.

Cora had stayed at the edge of groups, even when he urged her up beside him. "You afraid someone will listen to you?" he said on the way back to the motel. "That's what you're playing for."

"I don't know any of these people."

"Good time to practice. They don't know who to talk about."

She came out of the bathroom in a gray sweat suit and plopped on her bed.

"That outfit a guard against looking pretty?"

"I get cold at night."

"Good time to need a warm-up."

"Go to sleep, Pop."

He chuckled. That was easy. When he lay down, he said, "Did you bring a dress?"

"Skirt and blouse, for the dance."

"Would you let your hair down?"

A sleepy voice said, "Sure."

He couldn't sleep. He was director of his own stage play and he tried one role after another with Elizabeth. She silenced him every time.

⌣

"Now the way this'll go," Carl said, "is they'll call up the judges in order of seniority. I'll be the last performer, since I got at least ten years on Tucker and Phil. You won't have to say a word or do anything that'll embarrass you. You just follow me up there. 'Kansas City Kitty,' 'Hell Among the Yearlings,' and 'Sweet Molly's Waltz.' You know them all."

"What if Webb or Phil do one of those?"

"They won't. We already talked it over."

"But if they do?"

"Then I'll do another one you and me got tight as a drum. Don't you worry."

Dancers whirled and spun on the ground before the stage. People milled under the trees, headed for the toilets, lit cigarettes. Onstage, the young winners posed and hoedowned, short-bowed the shuffle, swungthatpartnerreel.

Carl liked Phil's style. He played it low key and dignified as far as posture, ripped out "Lost Indian" and modulated right into "Lady's Fancy," and then into "Oopic Waltz." People stood and yelled and clapped. More! More! More! But Phil acknowledged that he'd had his turn and done his stuff and he bowed from the waist and backed up for the announcer.

"WEBB TUCKER FROM TULSA, OKLAHOMA, GIVE HIM A HAND FOLKS!!!! YEAH, YEAH, YEAH, YEAH!"

"Now we move up," Carl said. "Right by the steps."

"I'm nervous."

"When aren't you? And you always do fine. I'd worry if you weren't worrying."

He knew the minute he heard the pickup notes, though they were the same for many songs. He knew because he saw Elizabeth at the edge of the dancers, with her face tilted up as if watching Webb, but she wasn't. She was watching Carl.

"That's 'Kansas City Kitty,'" Cora said. "Your tune." She was one step below him.

"Yep." He lit a cigarette. "Guess we know what's going to follow, don't we?"

"So what do we do? What are you going to play?"

He didn't answer because he couldn't. Some things you were never prepared for, like a man slapping a man. "I suspect we're not going to," he said, around the cigarette. "We'll see."

Webb had learned to clog somewhere along the road, and he spiced the turnarounds with a little heel clomping and leg throwing. People whooped, danced. Danced. This wasn't a contest, but a performance, no rules. Except courtesy. And that might be dead. Webb finally stopped, bowed, wiped his brow with a red bandana, and said something to his boys. His eyes swept to Carl, lighted, pinpoint blue-black jab. He went into "Hell Among the Yearlings."

"Another one of your tunes," Cora said. "He's a son of a bitch."

"Such language," Carl said, gratified that he could speak at all. "Let's go."

He stepped down behind Cora, waited while she slipped the guitar strap over her head and held the instrument up close. Then, holding fiddle and bow in his left hand, he steered Cora to the left of the dancers, heading toward the instrument cases. He had taken this path, the immediate one, with Cora along. Shame and pain were choking him from the inside, but he nodded politely to people he recognized. He'd lost every major battle in his life. Why should he be shocked now?

"That's the meanest thing I've ever seen," Cora said, and added an ugly word.

When he didn't answer right away, she started to turn around. He touched her shoulder to keep her headed forward. "Thought you were going to be a schoolteacher."

"God. I'm sick. Sick. Why doesn't somebody do something?"

"We are. We're walking out as graceful as can be."

"Play some other tunes. Outplay him with something. Anything. You can do it."

"Yes, I can. But I prefer to let what he did stand for what it is. Let his notes be the loudest he hears on this day."

Elizabeth was in the same spot, not even pretending to look at Webb. She was watching Carl steadily. He didn't change direction and he met her eyes the whole way. When he and Cora were directly in front of her, he stopped. "Elizabeth," he said, and she cocked her lovely head as if daring him.

"Yes?"

"Just thought I'd say that name one last time." He cleared his throat, spit to the side, then met her eyes again. "Enjoy your life." He turned to Cora and touched the rim of his hat. "We can continue now."

Cora kept looking over her shoulder. "Who was that?"

"No one you ever want to know."

From behind them he heard the low, plaintive beginning strains of "Sweet Molly's Waltz."

Cora stopped. "Does that woman have anything to do with the fiddler onstage?"

He couldn't answer.

"I'm going to knock her down." Cora spun around. He tugged her back, and by clearing his throat and gently nudging her forward, got them back on track. He was afraid she was crying for him. A new low.

Carl guessed maybe the world changed on a man without

175

his ever knowing it. He'd never known a judge not to get his due. He remembered having to stand when the judges played. His father had nudged him up. And the old crowds always got quiet at the beginning of each tune, like they wanted to hear that music, and *then* they danced, like the music just drew them out, made them sway to its rhythm. Maybe something was wrong with him as a person that he didn't get his due. Maybe he *did* get it. Maybe he was no more a fiddler than he was a man. Maybe he'd never been as good as he thought he was. Not in any way. In bed or onstage, he was an old fool.

Carl told Callie everything had gone well at the contest. "I enjoyed almost every bit of it, the judging, the young fiddlers, running into some of the Oklahoma crew. Made some good memories."

"Don't tell me you're considering moving back to Oklahoma."

"No. I like it better here. The air's cleaner." He stared into his coffee, not seeing it or anything, just gearing up. This should be an easy thing to say, but it took all his concentration to get force behind his words. "Fact is, I've been thinking maybe we should try living together."

Callie was in the middle of depositing dirty plates in her sink. She didn't rattle one, he noticed, but she did have a pleased look as she turned and came quickly over to him. She kissed him on top of the head. "I am *so* glad to hear that." She hugged his shoulders and pressed her cheek against his. "It'll be the best for both of us in every way."

"My friends will always be welcome though," he said.

"You mean Dolores?"

He hadn't realized a discussion might follow his simple statement. "I meant all my friends, but especially the music ones. I don't imagine Dolores will want to come by."

"But if she does?"

"Then you can talk with her too. Pretty interesting woman. Lost her job, house, kid. I wouldn't want her to lose friendships."

"You're right, Carl. Maybe she'd be interested in learning guitar. She could back me up."

Callie learned everything really quickly, but she didn't have the right spirit. He was suddenly very tired.

"You could keep this place for a month or two," he said, "just to see how it goes."

"Let's do it the other way round. Let's eat and sleep here. I'll have my studio and you'll still have your workshop and equipment. Meanwhile, we can look for a house that will accommodate both our crafts."

"Very practical," he said. "I just don't want to do it that way, Callie. We can take turns with the cooking. But you come to my bed." He had capitulated as much as possible for this moment.

"I'm happy to do that," she said, nodding crisply. "Thank you."

She comported herself very well, he thought. There was some give in her.

⌣

Dolores seemed to take it well, but then she'd been abandoned before, he guessed, by better people than he.

"I would've moved in with you," she said.

He feigned surprise. "You would have? Be a big waste of a good thing. You need a young stud. You got lots of good years left in you."

"Can we still be friends?"

"You bet."

"I can visit on Sundays?"

"If you don't, I'll come get you."

But she didn't visit and he didn't seek her out. He had made his decision. Had chosen. A bit of embarrassment there. And lonesomeness. He didn't want to cause trouble for either of them.

He stored some of his records and other paraphernalia at Callie's place, and exchanged some of his dishes and pans for hers—thus she could cook and eat as she was accustomed to. He threw away most of his ragtag clothing. He hadn't smelled Old English polish in years. Now his place gleamed and smelled like goodwomanatworkhere. She was a fine cook. She snored a little and didn't want much cover. And she was satisfied with a little petting.

"Sex will come about naturally as we learn more about each other," she said. "And if it doesn't, it won't matter."

It mattered to him, but he'd never been able to do anything about it.

⁂

Cora wanted to tell somebody about the terrible blow taken by Pop Bradshaw. She also wanted to write letters and make phone calls and soothe the incident totally out of Pop's life. And her own. Maybe, just maybe, he would've gone onstage anyhow with a different backup. If Amy had been there. Cora wished she could have shone for him and with him. It was her time, in a way, and she'd been saved from failing and saved from succeeding too.

"How did it go," Jack wanted to know, rather tentatively. She couldn't crumple against him, cry and moan. Maybe she couldn't crumple against any man. "Absolutely great," she said, sitting down in the chair across from the sofa where Jack was now settled. "He's a great fiddler. You have no idea. I didn't. I was so proud to be with him."

"So you did all right? Didn't get scared?"

"Of course I was scared. I shook all over."

"But you did all right?"

"Yes," she said. "Not as good as he did, but well enough."

"I'm glad to hear it." His voice was always deep, but now it had the husky fondness that could tear her apart. He cared about her, she believed, but he needed a young woman in his life. Someone who could match him in strength and fire and hope. He patted the sofa next to him and beckoned her with a come-here movement of his head.

She shook her head no.

The space between them was slight, only a couple of steps for him to be leaning close down over her, sliding his hands around her, and picking her up just enough to slide sitting beneath her, lowering her to his lap. He kissed her hair.

She felt his beard against her cheekbone, felt her warm, sweet breath. This was ageless. She felt a twinge in her heart. Hurt was on its way.

Amy

"Well, Dumpling," Will Vanderveen said, and won Amy's heart. She liked the line of his jaw. She liked his silence. She didn't care that no matter where he slid the bottleneck on that guitar, he was always a shade late and a shade flat or sharp. The very act of sliding was the most charming she'd ever seen. He kept cigarettes in his shirt's left pocket, and she liked that too. She wanted to pat the pack.

She hovered around him even when she was trying to play nonchalant.

"You just slow down, there," Pop Bradshaw told her. "You're acting as if he's silk and you're burlap. You're a good-looking gal and he'd better watch out. Adopt that way of thinking for a while."

"He's a physicist, Pop," she said. "He's a real brain and you'd never know it. He doesn't toot his own horn."

"You got this pretty skin, pretty little body, bright eyes, and loving ways. Seems to me he'd be getting the better end of the deal."

"We're not talking deals, here," she said. "That's a male perspective."

"Okay. Partnership. Relationship. How's that?"

"I'm not real refined, Pop."

"Bet he doesn't care a toot. And remember, lady, the man plays a Dobro. He's looking up to you, know it or not."

One night, when she had cooked dinner for him, she braved the remark "I'm not much of a homemaker." Will looked around the room, nodded, and resumed eating. That was an entire volume of rejection. She had *cleaned* the place before he came.

She worried about her past intimacies too, though she hadn't really been a loose woman. Bonnie had had more partners. Maybe Cora had too. Amy had never even promoted her own bosom. She sort of shrouded it. That was modesty, wasn't it? Sure. And she had never gone after a man. She didn't chase anybody. She just *was*. Will had changed her perception. Because he seemed so inexperienced or maybe just beyond the physical world—he even ate sparingly and absentmindedly—she felt tainted. She didn't believe she *should* feel that way, but there it was. She was going to make herself a servant in love if she didn't respect herself more. *Then act respectable,* she thought. *Be respectable.* That was different. Probably harder.

Jack

A cold February slicked the windows with rain. The backyard ran rivulets and Cora's dog came in shaking mud so
Cora cursed mildly and grabbed towels. Jack thought women
were amazing. They'd try to keep the house sunshine clean
in a blizzard. His mother hired a housekeeper to keep the
world shining while she went about her slow-paced but bril-
liant studies. Both his grandmothers rarely sat down. They
had turned paler and crisp clean with age. Cora had a
rougher go but the same instinct.

"Women try to defeat the elements," he told his father.

"They can too. But, oddly, I've not yet known a woman
who had an adequate self-image. They'll try anything believ-
ing they'll fail. Tell them they'll succeed and they're scared
to death."

"Cora's scared most of the time, anyhow," Jack said.

"Fear doesn't seem to stop her."

"No."

He drove up to The Mill, then changed his mind and
cruised the Tucson streets. He liked driving. He liked being on
the move. He liked being temporary. He thought maybe men
and women differed in that way. Men's lives were fleeting
and they knew it. Tucson was far too familiar to him for his
age. He mulled it over all afternoon, reading on Cora's sofa
while she graded papers. When she finished and sat rocking
in the maple chair, smoking, and—he knew—trying to dissi-
pate her irritation at his leisure, he said, "I've been thinking
that maybe I'll leave in June."

"June."

"Go to Virginia for a while. Then maybe Alaska. Lester has some friends with a lodge up there. They said I could play for the dinner crowd now and then."

"Okay," she said, and went in the kitchen.

He followed her, leaned in the doorway. She was rinsing out the coffeepot, filling it. "It's just a thought," he said. "I may not go. I won't if you don't want me to."

"No. That's okay. If you thought about it, it's time for you to go."

He was a little indignant but he tried not to sound it. "You're the one always saying we need to end this sometime."

She nodded. "I know. It's lasted longer than I thought it would." She removed the stove knobs, dropped them in the sink, and turned on the water. She reached for the soap. She still hadn't looked right at him. "We do need to end it. You just caught me by surprise, already knowing when and where. Sounds like planning."

"I haven't been planning. It just came to me."

"Okay."

"You through grading?"

"Yeah."

"Want to play for a while?"

A short laugh, not pretty. "No. Not now."

"You say we never jam."

"This isn't the day to do it."

Later, they made love. The rain droned over the house, the bedroom was afternoon-storm dark and warm. He loved her slowly and genuinely. He wondered briefly if maybe he'd never feel this way about someone else. He was pretty sure he would, though, and that made him both comfortable and guilty. He tried to make sure she climaxed, though she didn't always. He wanted their remaining time together to be as near perfect as he could make it. He finally realized that she had been crying, either during their lovemaking or immediately after.

"I'm sorry, Cora," he said. "I don't really want to go. I was just thinking about it and it seemed like a good idea at the time. Now it doesn't."

"No, it's a good idea," she said. "We'll plan on it and get ready."

The next morning she was a different woman. "I think you should go now," she said. "If we try to stay together knowing that you'll be leaving in a few months, things will change between us. I'll get resentful that you can go. All your little messes around here will aggravate me to death and I'll get bitchy. Before long, just to be able to bear it, I'll have to hate you or make you hate me. If you leave right away, things will always be the same. As much as they can be, I mean. There won't be a streak of bad times to remember."

"I don't think you mean what you're saying."

"I do. Maybe it's partly pride, but it's mostly common sense."

"So when should I plan on leaving?"

"How long will it take you to get ready?"

"I could go today."

She was silent one hard minute and he knew he'd been a fool. He'd hurt her.

"Then do it," she said.

He couldn't though. It took five days. He had to tell the crowd at The Mill that he'd be leaving and where he was headed. He had to get some money from the bank, get traveler's checks, have the truck given a good once-over. Had to have dinner at Josie's with her new boyfriend. Cora wouldn't go. Then Milosh offered to highlight him on *The Bluegrass Show* Saturday morning.

"This is an eclectic show," Milosh murmured into the mic. "And today we're featuring a rare breed, a rock musician who does bluegrass, country, and blues. Jack Martin, son of none other than Lester Martin the writer, whose *Lost Country* is just opening in town. Jack's leaving Tucson and headed *up north to Alaska, up north the race is on.* We're going to miss you, buddy. Who's going to lay a rock bass line behind my fiddle tunes?"

Jack picked "Nashville Skyline Rag," "Weave and Way," and "Jerusalem Ridge"; then he sang "Maybelline," "Hoochie Coochie Man," and "Illegal Smile."

Cora taped the show for him and he was surprised his voice didn't sound as good as he thought it did. His picking did though. He'd come a long way.

"Did you listen or just tape it?" he said.

"I listened. I kept thinking you'd dedicate a song to me. Stupid, wasn't it?" Then she was out of the room, in the bathroom, and he heard the shower going. When she came out she said, "I'm sorry. That wasn't called for."

He spent the afternoon drilling holes in her window frames so she could secure the windows with a nail when he was gone. He left her a gun too, and a box of shells.

"Men leave the funniest things," she said, but she wasn't being caustic. She seemed amused. After a minute, he thought it was funny too.

"Phallic symbols," he said.

"Lock the windows and pull out the gun. I get the message."

He left that night, which seemed wrong for travelers but right for men leaving women, because if they lay together one more night, no telling what shift in the world would occur by morning. She was smiling and seemed even a little cool. He thought it was the best time for her, so he loaded up his last bunch of stuff, his guitar and records. He left her some of the records.

He felt very guilty when he lifted the trunk his mother had given him. He and Cora had used it for a coffee table, and it was the most authentic, solid piece of furniture in the living room. He set it back down. "This looks better here than any place I'm going," he said. "You keep it."

"Your mother gave that to you. You take it."

"Nope. I want you to have it. It matters to me, like you do. I'll like thinking about it here."

That had been the absolutely right thing to do. She followed him outside. She chilled easily, and she kept her arms folded across her abdomen, except when he kissed her. Then she put her hands lightly on his chest and sort of patted the kiss over and done with. She was going to cry any minute.

"Bye, then," he said.

"Bye."

"Just for a while."

She nodded.

"I may be right back. I may not be able to bear this."

She nodded again. He didn't really want her to say anything anyhow.

"So, as your buddy Milosh says, off to Alaska." He opened the truck door. "Via Virginia and sundry states in between." He got in and closed the door, rolled down the window. "I love you, Cora. I mean that."

"I know."

Hearing her voice all guttural like that made him choke up. He didn't try to say more. He started the truck, tried to look lovingly and longingly at her, and drove away. He looked back in the rearview mirror but she was already out of sight. He thought she probably ran into the house.

It came to him about two hours later that he had developed a style of his own. He was always leaving at night.

He stayed at the Texas ranch a week all by himself, without even calling his relatives. He missed Cora. He called her every night at precisely 7:00 p.m. He kept getting the urge to go back, but he resisted it. Once she said, "You could come back if you wanted to," and he responded, "I know." That sort of hung there, telling for them both. He kept remembering that painful quiet when he could have said something nicer and didn't. This all proved Cora right though. Things got ugly if you tried to make them last past their natural ending. When he finally lit out for Virginia, he felt he owned the entire country and all of his future. He didn't tell anybody he was on the road again. He just took off. He decided he wouldn't hook up with another woman for about a year. He owed Cora that and it would prove the past two years hadn't been just a common older-woman, younger-man rutting-around situation.

$$\backsim$$

"Why don't you go jogging with me in the morning?" his mother said.

"Wait till eleven thirty and I'll do that." Jack thought his mother was a striking woman for her age. She was, in fact, a sensuous woman, a pale Ophelia but no whiner. He remembered a robe she had worn years ago and remembered his father at the typewriter. That explained their relationship. He thought maybe he was more physical than his father, maybe more like his mother.

"I'm not a jogger," he said. "Nor a scholar, nor a writer."

"Musician."

"We'll see."

"Let Lester help you."

"Maybe." He was going to be a man of few words. "First I'm going to Alaska."

He dallied. He played three weeks with a friend's band, drank a lot of beer, was the mysterious traveler—the latter pleased him. "Put inches on me," he told his dad, having mulled the phrase over first. His father's chuckle confirmed his wit. He drove back to Texas, back to Virginia again. He was waiting on May.

He didn't like Alaska but he liked having been there. He was putting many things behind him that some people would never reach in the first place. Maybe it was partly due to luck, to birthright, but surely he could lay some claim to daring and self-assurance.

Jack called Cora from the Tucson airport. She picked him up, wearing that pink blouse or one similar. She seemed shy to him. He hugged her and that was close to how he'd felt before, but not quite. They ate dinner at a restaurant and then she drove to her house. They talked about his mother and father, what he'd done over the summer in Alaska. Cora had driven clear to DC by herself and Milosh had flown there. They'd gone through the Smithsonian together, had seen Doc Watson perform. "He was great," she said. "So natural. We could have been sitting on his porch."

"Like kitchen musicians," he said, and recognized his own condescension.

"Not exactly."

"I wasn't putting him down. He's one of the best. Better than I'll ever be." She didn't argue. They had evened out.

"Lester's out at Josie's," he said. "We're going to drive to Texas together." He didn't want her thinking he might stay. There wasn't a chance of that anymore. He was very fond of her, but a bond had been broken. The fondness was akin to nostalgia, and almost painful to feel now. Being away had been easier. And would be again.

They ended up in bed, and Jack was amazed that he could enjoy sex with her the same as always, even better, knowing that he would be leaving in a few days. He thought that proved a point about the nature of men and women.

The next night Cora came back from the bathroom saying, "I think I have to go to the hospital."

He sat up and reached for his pants. He felt scared for her and irritated at the same time, as if she had done this deliberately.

"What's wrong?"

"A bladder infection, I think."

She called the emergency room and asked if she could just pick up a prescription until morning, and he was again amazed that she knew what to do. Where had she gotten this experience?

She went in the bathroom again and he followed her. She sat down and started to push the door closed but then her face contorted and she just went rigid. He thought she was dying or having a spell and the ugliness of her face at that moment startled and repulsed him. Then she relaxed. When she stood up, the water in the commode was all red, absolutely red, and there were drops of red on the inside of her thigh. He was terrified. "My God, Cora."

"It's just a bladder infection. You don't have to go with me."

"Of course I'm going with you." He didn't want to though. He wished he hadn't come to see her. But he wanted to help her too. The drama of this was overwhelming. How could they just lose blood like that and not be screaming through the streets?

He drove her car and at the hospital he walked right up to the counter with her. He was going to fill out the papers for her, if necessary.

"Go sit down over there," she said.

"Nope."

"Please."

He did, but he watched her in case she needed anything.

He thought blood might come rushing down to the floor any minute but the nurse didn't seem perturbed. He heard every question they asked her.

"When was your last period?"

"I had my uterus removed eight years ago," she said.

He took a magazine then and pretended to have been reading all along. He felt gutted himself.

Later, when she emerged from the examining room, she had two bottles of pills.

He knew she was embarrassed. She was so much in control, looking past him with a smile instead of at him. "That's a scary thing, Cora," he said. "If it happened to me, it would frighten me to death. You really behaved well."

"Not much choice, actually," she said.

He lay awake by her all night, feeling that she was going to erupt into something unpleasant and he was on the edge of it. The bedroom was the smallest in his experience or at least that he remembered.

He left the next morning. His father picked him up in a rented car and they drove out of Arizona, into New Mexico, headed for the Texas ranch house.

"I thought she was dying," Jack said, "but it was a traumatized urethra. That's what she told me. She was embarrassed."

"You seem to have handled it nicely. It must have been unpleasant for both of you."

Jack agreed with his father that women didn't have an easy time of it.

⁓

In Texas, he met his next woman. She was older too, but she didn't tend toward being a victim. His father had given a reading, and the woman was a guest at the reception. She had thick black hair, eyes more violent than Josie's.

When Jack played at a rally a month later, there she was

again. He couldn't mistake her touches. He just went home with her, and there he was, captured. She was forty. She was hot. She was nothing like anything he had imagined happening to him, or more like everything he had imagined. He wished she weren't forty.

"These things happen," his father said. "Don't worry about it."

Jack got cast in a miniseries of his father's book. During the filming, the woman stayed with him in the hotel and on the set. He got sick when anyone was near her or when he couldn't see her. He felt like a hot wire ran right from her to him, but he never let her know that. Even before he saw himself on-screen, after cuts and cuts, he knew he was no actor. He had excellent taste and could tell the real actors.

Still, he was in no hurry with any of it. He was enjoying himself. Then one morning he woke up and he was ready to go. He thought he would change his mind, but that didn't happen.

The evening after he moved out, she came into the bar where he was playing and sat at a table alone. He was rougher onstage now, used his drawl for the jokes, and the audience was responding better to him. When his break came, he didn't join her, just stayed onstage and rearranged his setup. During the first tune of the next set, she stood up.

"You self-righteous little prick," she yelled. She threw a beer bottle at the stage, but it fell short. He managed to put his guitar on the floor and get to her before she threw another bottle. She was wearing a short black skirt and white silk blouse. Right as he neared her, she stepped back and jerked the blouse open. Her breasts swung free, the nipples erect and almost black.

"Anyone want to take over for this kid?" she yelled. "Anyone think he can handle me?"

Jack dragged her toward the door and two men came up

to stop him, but she called them names and leaned into Jack. The minute they were on the sidewalk, though, under neon and struggling in night air streaked with jukebox music, she slapped him three times, sharp, cracking loud. He slapped her back, and then wound up in her bed. They left the bed only to use the bathroom or get something to eat. The second evening, when she was asleep, he showered, dressed, went to his new place where nothing was even put away, and loaded it all, except his guitar, into the back of his truck. With the guitar in the passenger seat, he drove to Nashville, chain-smoking, feeling burnt up and soiled. He felt like he was at the end of a dream, right on the edge of waking up and finding the real room of his life around him.

His father flew in to see him and they talked about women and books. Jack asked Lester if he'd ever struck a woman and his father said no, though he had wanted to.

It was impossible, Jack thought, for Lester to have penned the lives he did and not to have felt the emotions he expressed. He subdued them, absorbed them through his heart into his brain and created with them. Jack needed a quicker medium.

"I think I'm a wild man," he said.

"That runs in the family," Lester replied. "You were intensely provoked. But I hope nothing like that happens again."

"It was reflex. She hit me a number of times and I just swung out."

"Kindness is a reflex too," his father said. "You remember that and try to stay calm enough to think before you act. There are different means of being manly. Different kinds of bravery too. Just like talent."

⌣

His father financed good recording equipment, and Jack

gradually met some decent songwriters and musicians. "You're damned good," one man told him. "Stop thinking like a kid. Sell your lyrics, don't just sing them."

He was between trips, at the ranch house. It was a fall day, the oil rig like a stark reminder of the differences between generations in his family. The front and back doors were open and wind swept through pleasantly. The walls were lined with books, books. Three beer bottles were on the rough dining table along with a filled ashtray, a small metal one, fake gold. The wall phone rang, jarred the hell out of him. He got it on the third ring, expecting a family member's voice, but what he heard was soft and immediately recognizable though she said only "Jack?"

Cora.

"Yeah. How are you?" A stupid phrase, he thought, but standard. It was what someone said to a call out of the blue. He could feel the presence of her, the intensity and anxiety of her. It was frightening even now, with the hollow house around him, and him situated in another life. Entirely. "How you doing?" he said, feeling kindly and loving toward her just as suddenly as if he'd fallen in love or lust again. None of it true. And all of it.

"I'm glad I caught you. I wanted to tell you about Michael."

"What about him?"

"I don't want to say it, but . . . there's no way to say it better. He's dead, Jack. He shot himself."

Of course, Jack thought. That was it. Michael had been headed that way all along. That's what was in his music. Maybe they'd all had a brief, intense time together because it was going to happen. "I'm sorry to hear it," he said, genuinely sorry for Michael and for the loss of Michael. "When?"

"Two days ago. Milosh called me yesterday. I couldn't decide whether to call you."

"I'm glad you did."

"I don't know any more. I'm in Missouri now. I won't be going back."

"What are you doing there?"

"Teaching. My mother lives close. I can finally spend time with her."

"I guess that's good."

"Yes. It's the goal I set for myself, at least."

There were a few more small words, mostly about Michael, the pity of it, the loss, every word saying the same thing, floating in the distance between them now, until they said good-bye.

He had one more beer, thinking about Michael's songs and about Cora. How she looked one night in the dark bedroom. She was so slender and fair. Unreal now, more real. He didn't give a good goddamn about anything except getting out of the house and away from this unbearable pain and guilt. Every human being in the world should be able to be happy.

When Jack flew to California to see his father, he took along a good demo tape of his own songs. "Give this to someone," Jack said. "I want to get this show on the road."

Five months later, his first album was out, and he had met a young woman named Cynthia. She wasn't a musician but she liked listening as long as he didn't forget she was there. She was tall and tan, with black hair down to her waist. He was twenty-three and so was she. He became slightly ashamed that his first two women had been older and for a while he let go of any of the good memories of Cora. They were sullied by association with ugliness between then and his present life. Sometimes, though, he'd remember a song she sang or a story she told. He thought what it must have been like to live in that small town with a riverman alcoholic father, how she must have felt to go door to door asking the residents if they had a piano.

On a summer night, after a gig and on the way to another

one, Jack sat at an old student's desk in a motel room with a chintzy green-shaped lamp providing a cone of light, and he penned a song for Cora. Then he sat on the bed with his guitar and he coaxed out the blend of thought and sound. He sang it over and over till it was perfect. For him, perfect, and maybe for her. She'd hear it someday, he believed. She had always wanted him to dedicate a song to her. She'd recognize that he had finally done it, and in a better fashion. He had truly listened to the stories she shared.

Amy and Will

"I want to go with you, Will," she said, and he came up with all these genuine objections: that he'd be starting a new job; that he had no family or friends to keep her occupied; that the money he'd be making wasn't as much as she seemed to think it was; that the winters, so he'd heard, were terribly hard on newcomers.

"A guy I worked with said half his salary went to heating bills."

"I don't care. I want to go. I'll pay my own way. And if it doesn't work out, I'll pay my own way back too. I'll get a job just as soon as we get there."

She taped all the songs she wanted to keep and then sold the albums. She had sold the bass to Cora for a hundred dollars less than Paul Welford offered her. "I want a woman to own it," she told Cora. "Don't tell Paul what you paid for it."

Will hadn't yet said I love you. He just went along with her plans like he was fond of her.

"You do want me to go, don't you?" she said.

"If I say yes, then I'll be responsible for you. You have to make up your own mind what you want to do."

Oh, he was reasonable, so logical. She was quivering to death from his steadiness. Her shoulder hurt all the time as if someone had wrenched it behind her for years.

"Partly from playing the guitar, I'm certain," her chiropractor said, "but largely tension. You also have that extra weight." He nodded discreetly at her breasts.

"Thank goodness," she said, "since I'm missing other assets."

Big Bob gave them a farewell party and she was swimming in nostalgia. She loved this dry dead brown high sky sweeping prickly coyote jackrabbit sturdy cactus country. She played rhythm and lead like she'd seamed the whole valley. And maybe nothing in her life would ever be this good again. But a person had to charge ahead and just grab whatever good popped up before it disappeared and this Will Vanderveen was the best thing that had ever happened to her. She was happy just knowing he was on the planet.

They were on their way back to town when Will said, "I know it's probably none of my business what you did before you met me, but I wonder if you've slept with most of the men that we jammed with tonight."

"No," Amy said. She knew she should say something more, maybe the truth, but she wasn't going to ruin her life because of one yes or no. She brushed at her skirt, hummed one of the songs they had played, and tapped her hand against the seat. When he didn't say anything for a mile or so, she said, "You been with a lot of women?"

"Welford said you and your friend Cora were easy to tune."

"Wishful thinking," she said. A little while later, city lights spinning across the windshield, she said, "Cora called Paul a 'peach-orchard boar.'"

"I'm not sure what that means," Will said, "but I can guess."

Amy put her hand on his thigh. She wanted to ask him again about women, but she didn't dare open up the subject. "I've heard," she said, "that people in Massachusetts are real quiet. You'll fit right in."

She thought he wasn't going to answer at all, which she was getting used to, but in a moment he said, "Well, you'll get them talking, won't you?" He glanced at her and smiled. He had the most absolutely lovely smile. Slow and shy. The most winning smile she'd ever seen.

"You sold your Dobro?" Amy said.

"Yes. Before we ever left Tucson."

"I thought you liked music."

"I do. I'm just not very good at it and I won't have time for it for a while, and I thought the money'd come in handy."

"But now we can't play together."

"We never could, Amy. *You* could."

She got a job with a surveying company, which paid well enough that she wanted to pay half the expenses, but Will wouldn't let her. "No more than one-fifth," he said. She was amazed that he was willing to support her totally. She paid the one-fifth and put everything she could into savings. When and if Will did need something, she'd have the money for it.

She played alone, with records sometimes, and kept the sound low because he was a quiet man and read or thought a great deal.

"You don't have to be quiet, Amy," he said one day, as if he only then had become conscious of her restraint. "Your music doesn't bother me at all."

She played louder after that, almost joyously. But alone. And notes alone eventually get sad and slow. She was so fiercely hungry for jam sessions, her body ached. She was starving. Even the air was missing something.

At a music store she asked about local jams and on a Thursday night drove to the community center where the old-time fiddlers met. About twenty people were there. She was thrilled. One group was beginners. All the people knew each other. They looked her over, and one man, the president of the club, greeted her. He explained the setup and gave her a card. They split up, much like at The Kettle, only it was in a country with snow locking out the world. Coats were piled on two of the long tables against the wall. The musicians had on heavy shoes. Amy joined an old-timey group of five people and took out her guitar. The musicians looked at the instrument and her, and they nodded at least a tiny degree. "That's a D-28," one man said, silver-haired, holding a reddish fiddle. Amy thought he'd say more but that was it. They were all men except for a thin young girl fiddler they called Tessa. The girl smiled shyly at Amy.

"Growling Old Man," another man said, and in seconds, without calling the key, he started into it. Amy knew it, and was glad she did. She held back a little, reading the cues of whether or not a guitar player was allowed to take a break. No. Not this first song. One fiddler after the other. When it came to Tessa, and she was ending her turn, she dipped her head a little toward Amy but Amy, with the merest movement and lowered eyelids, signaled "Not yet."

After three more tunes the silver-haired fellow asked her, "You got one?"

Amy called "Ragtime Annie" because for sure everyone would know that and she wouldn't be asking for attention. There were rules. She worried about what to say if one of them asked if she was married. They'd want to know why her husband wasn't along. No one asked that night. When the question came at another jam, she said, "He plays country."

✥

Amy scooted off the examination table while the doctor was writing in her file.

"I think we should plan on a cesarean," he said.

"Why? What's wrong with me?"

"You have a very narrow pelvis. A cesarean would be safer for you and the baby."

Amy read his expression, looking for another judgment.

"That's the only problem I see," he said. "Now if you want

200

to try for a natural birth, we can. You'll have to keep the baby's weight down, and your own."

She wasn't going to starve her baby starting out. What a terrible thought.

"I'll have the cesarean. I don't mind. I'm not afraid."

"You looked worried."

"I thought I might . . . have something . . . transmittable."

"I see. Well, how about a full lab workup to ease your mind?"

No doubts. "Yes. Please."

He scribbled in the file. "All right, then. Sandy will be in here shortly to draw some blood. She'll give you a packet too, on prenatal care of mother and child."

On the way home she talked to the baby in there. "I'm taking care of you," she said. "Your momma will keep everything ugly in the world away from you."

For the next two days she thought of the lab tests only in darts, and each time shivered. Finally, she sat down in an old rocker she had found at a junk store. She was in a sun shaft in her own living room, Will outside shoveling snow off the steps.

What if she had something dire that could really harm the baby? Would she . . . kill another one? She began weeping at the very idea and made herself consider it fully, all the while hearing the sounds of Will's caretaking. Her face was wet with tears. She had to find a box of tissues, and as she passed the phone table, the phone rang. She knew it was the doctor's office just because her fate meant it was. It was the doctor himself, not the nurse.

"Ms. Chandler?"

She was clean! A clean woman! Deep breaths. Sweet baby! Happiness.

Will carefully scraping his shoes, standing on the rug inside the door to unlace them and leave them on newspaper to the side of the rug.

"You crying, Amy? What's wrong?"

Nothing. Kiss him. "I have some good news. I think it's good."

Will thought they had best get married and they did so, by a justice of the peace. Amy wore a pink wool suit and pink shoes. She didn't know why she loved him. It was the set of his jaw, the line of his shoulders, the taper of his fingers, the smile, smile, smile. She did love that man. Will Van der Veen, Will Vanderveen. Amy and Will Vanderveen.

⌣

Amy saw the baby lifted out. Saw that precious wriggling pale wonder lifted right out of her own belly. "Is he okay?" she said. "Is he okay?"

Perfect, they assured her then and later and later.

"I didn't know you were so worried something would be wrong," Will said. He was seated by her bed, holding her hand.

She wanted to name the baby Josh Watson Crary Blake Vanderveen.

Will wanted to think about that awhile.

The Kettle

The Kettle was closing. After how many years? Who remembered? The place opened in the sixties, to give young people a wholesome place to hear music—no drugs. Hah! Didn't they ever check the stairwells? Hell, they could've just taken a deep breath out in the parking lot. The sixties. Sometimes people read poetry, stuff like that. Yeah. And once a woman danced with a snake. No way. Well, that's the story. Closing, huh? It'll reopen. Maybe. Someone said a new business is coming in, something technological, maybe connected to the university and science. Oh. Well, times come and go.

On the final Friday night someone turned the donation can upside down. Someone else taped a piece of ribbon on the can. Musicians converged as if for a concert of known stars. Most of them felt like family, already nostalgic for home though they hadn't left yet. They were warm to one another, more respectful than at any time in their lives. The kitchen volunteers made only coffee, kept the pot full, but let people serve themselves. It was early fall, and both the front and back door remained open, air and music sweeping through from the parking lot, walks, stairwells, rooms. No corner was left unattended. Music could have been holding the building together.

Stage acts, brief so everyone could play, moved fluidly on and off to generous and sincere applause.

A middle-aged man got onstage, finger-plucked nice, funky blues, and sang a crude song about sucking a cigar.

"A new guy, I guess."

"Apparently."

They applauded anyway.

A heavyset woman sang "Muleskinner Blues." Most of the audience remembered an old fat guy who sang the hell out of that song. Gary somebody, played with a male fiddler named Shirley.

No matter who went onstage, they brought to mind someone else, so that the rooms seemed richly crowded.

When Molly O'Rourke stood before the mic alone, people first glanced around for Pete, then hushed one another, because Molly was a timid woman with a soft voice.

"Didn't Milosh bail Molly out of some money problem? What was it I heard? Just recently."

"She was having her car repossessed."

"That's it. He paid the lien."

"But she's paying him back."

"Are they a couple?"

"No. Maybe. Who knows? He helps anyone who asks."

The girl didn't sing. She fiddled, first a plaintive tune. "The Water Is Wide," someone said, or close to it, with high notes sounding almost, almost, like a woman crying, and beneath them the drone of a low string, a male undertone.

"She is good, isn't she?"

"On those Celtic pieces, you bet."

When Molly stepped down, they watched Milosh take the stage, adjust the mic, and stand solemnly silent. They appreciated the big guy's attitude. A common memory was being set—the candles flickered over checkered tablecloths, cast silhouettes larger than life. Through the mic came Milosh's announcer's voice, the one they could recall as firm and sure. "Well, buddies, I could say a lot, as usual, but what's done is done, and The Kettle is over. I'll keep it sweet, short, and simple. We made history. People talk about the good old days, long for the good old days. We were, and are this minute, the good old days. Let's all get up here and play one song together."

"In the same key, Milosh?"

"Small detail. Small detail."

Pop Bradshaw had appeared, which was rare lately, and he stood off to the side of the stage, more somber than usual, holding the fiddle close to his cheek as he checked the tuning and waited for the others. Some people got instruments, some meandered into the back room for a last visit, some out into the night because they didn't like farewells. Inside, though, was still a decent crowd, enough to satisfy a musician onstage, and, since they were all musicians, enough to satisfy each other. They played together, onstage and off, played more than one tune, going from one to another as if the medley might not end, might weave every song ever written together and go all the way around the world.

Cora

Cora went into Mason's one music store and read the thumb-tacked notice on the corkboard. Paper notes and strips of phone numbers fluttered like tiny wings.

"Can I help you?" a burly, bearded guy asked, standing with his hands clasped behind him. He reminded her of a boy she had known in grade school named Jim Darling, an impossible name.

"I'm looking for open jams or open mics. I'm a mediocre musician so nothing very competitive. I just like to play."

"You want to put a note on the bulletin board?"

"Yes, I do."

He gave her a notepad and a ballpoint pen. Spare thumb-tacks were in a corner of the board.

She thought of weird people calling her but wanted to risk it anyhow.

Singer and guitar player (medium level) looking for a jam.

She tore up the note because she hadn't said *a woman* and didn't want to say it.

The friendly clerk came up. "There's an open jam at the American Legion on Thursday nights. It's mostly older people. There's another one near Clinton, bluegrass, on Fridays."

"Could you tell me where exactly in Clinton?"

In a metal building just off Highway 50, right after road N junction.

That Friday, she gave her dog supper, two treats, left the radio playing softly, and carried guitar, then bass, to the car. It was a cool night, dark clouds low, like a fleet of something coming in. The desert sky had been always high. If she got lost here, in her home country, she would wind up in black woods and winding roads, and air so humid she'd smother above ground. She found the metal building: a glowing rectangle with lighted windows and a few cars and trucks scattered in the parking lot. It was difficult getting the bass out of her car because she had to lift the bottom up over the lock mechanism, turn the bass sideways and scoot it out until she could grasp part of the neck. It was to her a gentle responsibility. Having the bass was like going in on the arm of a friend. She maneuvered it through the open door and a string-bean guy came over to help.

"Oh looky here. Do we need you, lady! Hey, fellows! We got a bass player!"

She wasn't that good yet but she was going to be.

She felt so wonderful, so damned wonderful. The woods, the towns, everywhere, were filled with musicians. She was one of them. Maybe not talented, but one of them nonetheless. Sort of an orphan musician. Not of the tribe, but adopted.

Amy

Two months before the national flat-picking contest, Amy reserved a motel room in Winfield. She even sent a money order in advance, because she didn't want Will to see a charge slip and she couldn't afford a mix-up when the whole world would be crowding in for the contest. A single woman could always find a place to sleep, but a married woman/ mother had to think of more than rest.

She had played with records more than with people the last three years, but she still liked the East. She liked the gradual dense falls, trees exploding into color, skies crimping up against the cold. She and Will lived in a big wooden house and Will kept it HOT. And oh, she loved that Will Vanderveen. He could keep an engine in the living room for all she cared. She didn't need to go out much, but she missed jam sessions. She wasn't invited to many. She met people at fairs and concerts, but people in the East didn't see you, Will told her, till you'd lived there long enough they'd forgotten you came from somewhere else. There was nothing impromptu and close. An open jam occurred just forty-five miles away on the first Thursday of each month, but the musicians played only for the contra dancers who showed up. How many tunes they played, what speed, and how long, depended on the dance group. It wasn't fun enough to warrant leaving Will home alone, even though he said he wouldn't mind. He wouldn't come along, and why should he? He had no desire to become one of the dancers.

She had kept her eyes open for someone like herself, fired

up about music, someone itching to play really, really well, to play a tune almost beyond reach, and to perform at least now and then. It was too long coming. So she played mostly with her tapes. She'd sit on the floor cross-legged, and she'd pick along with Doc and Merle Watson, Dan Crary, Josh White, Mark O'Connor, Norman Blake. *Bluerailroadtrainblackberry blossomlonesomejennydoc'sbreakdownblackmountainragJerusalem ridgestoneycreeksaltcreekshadygroveopenupthempearlygates*

⌣

Amy packed a suitcase with disposable diapers and jars of baby food, and then put the suitcase back in the storage room. She considered telling Will about Winfield. She didn't believe he would ask her to stay home. He might offer to take time off and come with her—which, admittedly, she didn't want. He might suggest she hire a sitter. Thinking in this manner made her physically uncomfortable, agitated and tense. She wanted simply to go and play and not talk about it. She would always be a good wife, work at contentment for Will and for herself. She would be rid of the niggling need to play before people, to watch the glow of the music above everyone, even her. She would have met one of her own goals and could settle down. Could say, *There. I stayed with it all the way. I played at the hardest level.* She wouldn't let herself think past the act of competing, wouldn't indulge a daydream of winning. No. Just the act. If she had to endure unpleasantness later, all right.

A piece of sunlight unfolded on the kitchen floor, like a note, and it startled her. She recalled George telling her that she reasoned to get what she wanted and feel right about it. She dwelt on that a few seconds.

The morning of her flight to Winfield, she called Will at

work. "My dad's in the hospital," she said, crossing two fingers and wrapping them around the phone cord. "He's okay now, stable, but Mom's called in a ticket for me. She's staying at the hospital too. She wants me to come out there for a couple of days, to spell her and help out. I'll call you tomorrow night. You won't even know I'm gone."

"Should I take off and stay with Josh?"

"Of course not. Josh is coming with me. I can take this baby anywhere. You'll enjoy a little time alone."

The baby's name, shortened by Will, was Joshua Watson Vanderveen and he was sun, moon, and stars above all the good things in her life. He was perfect, unblemished, fat and ugly, with straight wild hair that wouldn't lie down, a sloppy wet grin, and he nursed her breasts with gusto, all noise and appetite. Now, as she wiped jam from his cheeks and hands, he slapped at nothing and made a sound of his own, a cross between a gurgle and a laugh.

"We're going picking," she whispered toward his broad face.

⌣

The Winfield sky was wide-high-blue, the air fresh. She could be tromping from camp to camp, slipping into jam sessions and surprising the hell out of everyone. But she sat in the center of her motel bed that afternoon and played her first-round songs over and over and over.

"Like that, Joshua? Like that, sweet thing? So does Momma."

When he slept, she sat on the bathroom floor, where she could see if he moved, and again played the songs over and over so the sound reverberated and she heard every nuance.

She called Will. She could imagine him in the house, only one light on in the entire place. He didn't mind dark or silence. "Dad's fine," she said. "He's going home tomorrow. Josh is sleeping. He's a good little traveler."

She slept peacefully. She dreamed about music, that she opened her fists and notes flew away like hummingbirds.

She took a cab to the campgrounds, a halter securing Josh against her breasts. Hum, hum, hum. Oh happy day.

This wasn't how she had planned to be at Winfield. She had planned to be single, to knock them dead and wind up on the road with a good band.

She drew number eight. She liked that number. It was a good circle number, all tight and firm.

She didn't watch the other contestants, because that was bad luck. And she tried not to listen, because what if she heard someone outplay her? Better never to know who it was until later, if ever.

When they called her number, she had her guitar in one hand, Josh and a blanket in the other.

"Let me hold him for you," the announcer said.

"He'll be okay. He likes music."

"You got a backup?"

"No."

"We got a standby."

"No. I'm used to playing alone."

She spread the blanket in front of the mic, sat Josh in the center. People, people, people. Yells. She sat down in the chair, looked right at her baby's face. "You listen to Momma," she said. "This is going to be good."

She *was* good. The best she'd ever been. She heard the quiet pause before the explosion of yells. She had made the first cut. Now she'd play tomorrow morning. Oh, the crowd was tempting. Pats on her back, handshakes, smiles, invitations to pick awhile. "I got to get him out of the sun," she said. "He's real fair like his dad."

She got a cab back to town, had the cabby drive through

the fast-serve of a hamburger place. She ate in her room. At suppertime she called Will. He didn't answer. That worried her and she drew her fingers to her mouth. That night she practiced her best tunes. Over and over and over. "Sally Johnson," "June Apple," "Dusty Miller," "Elzic's Farewell." She fell asleep in her clothes, stretched out on the bed beside Josh. When the phone rang, she thought she was at home. She heard Will's voice. "Amy?" he said. When she said "Yes," there was this chasm of silence. Then he hung up. She dialed home immediately but he didn't answer. She couldn't sleep then. The room turned foreign and ugly, and all her music sour as sin. She didn't want to hurt anybody or worry anyone. Especially not Will. Never him. She was lying in the midst of roiling clouds. She had to pay for this. This would have to do her for a lifetime. "I just wanted to enter once, Will," she said as if he were in the room with her. "What if I can win?"

◡⋰

She played fourth. Oh, the sun was bright and the crowd liked her baby on the blanket. Amy picked the strings to make Josh's lips bubble pleasure. Her face grew warm and the sun glinted haloes everywhere she glanced. She smiled. Her fingers danced sadness and joy at being there but being there in the wrong. Music winged from her hands, flew over the crowd, got all caught up being light in the breeze, and faded away, faded away, faded away.

She took second place. Second in the whole country. Amy Chandler, folks, originally from San Diego, California, via Tucson, Arizona, and Bethany, Massachusetts. Amy, come on up here and bring that baby with you.

◡⋰

"Your momma plays the guitar, Josh," she said on the plane. "Yes she does. And she'll teach you. You'll be the best in the world. You'll pick circles around the stars."

The taxi driver carried the suitcase to her front porch. No light was on. Dry leaves bunched at the edge of the walk. A wind had blown over the chair on the porch.

"Daddy's asleep," she said. "Yes he is. So we'll be very quiet, right? We'll just go to bed, you and me." She unlocked the door and carried Josh and the guitar inside. She held her breath. She'd ache forever if he was gone. She turned on a lamp.

His books were on the shelves. A half-full glass was on the coffee table.

She was utterly grateful.

"Momma loves you, Josh. You're the sweetest baby ever made."

She stopped at the first bedroom. Will lay on his stomach, one arm thrown over her side of the bed. She carried the baby to the next room and nursed him in the dark. She loved Will Vanderveen. She padded into the bathroom and showered.

When she moved Will's arm, he turned on his side. She slipped in beside him, lay very still.

In a little while he said, "How'd you do?"

"Pretty good. I took second place." His breathing stayed even, and his body didn't tense up. He wasn't a harsh or vengeful man and that was why, all the more, she shouldn't have hurt him. She put her hand on his chest. "Don't be mad, Will. Please."

"You have to know I was angry," he said. "You scared your mother too. I called her. Then I called every hotel and motel in Winfield."

"How did you know where I was?"

"Where else would you go? Second, huh? Out of how many?"

"Fifty-four. I didn't want to talk about it beforehand. I was afraid something would happen to it."

"I can almost understand that."

She felt the comfort of him just in the tone of his voice. "I won't ever have to do it again."

"Think you could take first?"

She curled up next to him. Plans were willy-nilly amid the surprises of life. Will Vanderveen was still the best surprise, better than any plan. She loved that man. Yes she did.

Carl

Carl dreamed a woman's scream. It was piercing and long-holding so he had time to open his eyes and realize where he was before it faded away. Callie slept on. He rolled over, grunted at the lack of space, and closed his eyes. Then another scream, a god-awful sound, and a male voice booming back. Carl headed for the closet, jerked his pants from the hanger, and struggled into them in the hallway. He opened the front door while he was zipping them up.

"Carl?" came from the bedroom behind him. "Carl? Where you going?"

Now the man's voice filled the night air. "Come on. Come on, you damned crazy bitch. You just try to take one more step on my property."

Carl ran down the steps and across the rough desert grass barefoot. Maybe six people milled around outside one small house. A fat man dressed in Bermuda shorts and a sweat shirt was at the fore, his head jutted forward like an old turtle. A few feet in front of him a woman straightened up from the ground. "I mean it," the guy yelled. "I don't care if you are a woman. You come near me, and I'll knock the hell out of you again."

Dolores. She was in a white nightgown with her dark hair all thin, wild around her pointed face. She raised her arm, the hand fisted, and her face became shadowed. She looked like a little kid roused from sleep.

"What's going on here?" Carl asked, though he knew exactly what had happened and would happen.

"Who're you?" from the angry man. "Oh. It's you. She's at it again, that's what. Come walking into my house a few minutes ago like it was hers, talking about God. Scared the shit out of my wife."

Dolores was babbling now, with her arm still raised. Her tone seemed rational, but the stream of words didn't connect. Carl wasn't even sure they were words, except for the occasional "God." That word she said just as clearly as if she were a prophet.

"I'll get her inside," he said.

"She'll just come right back. You know that as well as I do. I'm going to call the police."

"Don't do that, mister. She's not the kind of person that should go to jail."

"I'm warning you," the guy said, and glanced at Carl. "Get her out of here. You better get her out of here."

Carl didn't have time. Dolores ran right at them and the guy just swung, openhanded, as if she were a bag of dirt and it didn't matter how he connected. She fell, plop and pathetic, all white and struggling up like she had a good cause here and wouldn't stay down. The man had straddled her. He was going to hit her again.

"She's sick," Carl spat. "She's sick, can't you see?" He grabbed the man's arm and jerked him. The guy straightened up. "Get away from her," Carl said. "I'll get her."

"I'm going to call the cops. I've had it with her." He turned toward the group and his house.

Carl tried to raise her up, but she fought him too, twisting around and almost as heavy as he, and he wound up falling down with her. She screamed and wouldn't stop. He rolled over and straddled her and clamped one hand over her mouth. He felt something wrong there. The jaw just gave. Broken. "You poor crazy creature," he said. "He hurt you bad. Hush, Dolores. You hush now. Someone's coming and we'll go get some rest."

Callie came up and bent down. "Can you get her in the house?"

"The police are on the way. I don't want anybody else to hurt her and I don't want her to hurt herself."

"I'll get her robe."

She came back in a minute.

"Just drop it there," Carl said. "I'll cover her when we can both stand up."

The police had to fill out their papers. Carl wouldn't get up till the paramedics were ready to hold her. He wasn't going to let any policemen subdue her. People hadn't cleared out, they had just spread out, lingering in the shadows. He went back to his place. "They're going to take her down to county, so I'm going too," he said.

"You can't do anything else."

"That's not the point."

Callie had fixed coffee. She was still in her robe. Peach corduroy, sashed and prim. He didn't know how she could look right all the time. He was trembling a little and he sat down on the arm of the sofa to have a cigarette. He put on a white shirt and a black string tie. He put on his good boots and a black hat.

"I want them to know she's got decent friends," he said.

"I'll come with you," Callie said.

"Don't need to. One of us should get some sleep."

He just hung around in the hospital parking lot till the police were gone, then went into the waiting room. "I'm here for Dolores Nelson," he said. "If she needs anything, you let me know."

"There's no need for you to wait. She's sedated now."

"I'll be right over there."

He sat where a huge window looked out on the freeway overpass. Car lights arced over it like slowly shooting stars.

He had gone outside for his second cigarette when Callie drove up. He grunted, watched her park.

"How is she?" she asked.

"I don't know. They said they sedated her, but I heard her yell twice. Takes a while when she's off like that."

"Why didn't you just come on home?"

"Oh, who wants to lie in a hospital with nobody waiting?"

"That's not your responsibility."

"No. 'Tisn't." He cleared his throat and turned to spit a little.

Callie came inside with him and sat in a chair opposite. She looked through a couple of magazines. The sun came up. Big crimson line along the horizon, the overpass now a gray functional curve. It looked as much like sunset as sunrise, the only difference his own sense of time and direction. "You better go on back," Carl said.

"You coming?"

"When I hear what the doctor has to say."

She left.

They let him visit Dolores around noon. He carried a cup of weak coffee in with him. "Had a time last night, didn't you?" he said. She didn't answer and he was glad enough. He could tell from her eyes what might break through.

"I can't keep up with her," he told the doctor. "But she needs somebody."

The second day, they moved Dolores to the fourth floor. Carl went by after work. He did the talking. Her eyes were dull but not trusting. You couldn't infuse trust with a pill or an injection. Somewhere inside her the wild heart wanted to protect itself. When he was ready to leave, he stood at the foot of her bed and let his hand hover over her foot like he wanted to pat her, which he did. "I'll be back tomorrow. If you need anything, and can write it down, I'll be glad to get it for you. I'll ask the nurse on my way out."

She was watching his hand. He raised it slightly, in farewell. "Tomorrow."

The third evening, stepping into his house, he knew

something had changed. Callie had supper on the table. She was dressed in spring colors. Her yellow shirt had red and blue and green zigzag borders around collar and cuffs, almost an Indian look, just not quite.

"Steamed squash, sautéed salmon, and sliced tomatoes," she said. "How's Dolores?"

"Better. She won't talk, but that's probably good. I suspect she's not ready to make sense."

When he hung up his coat and hat in the bedroom, he saw her clothing had been removed from the closet. He opened one of the dresser drawers she used. Empty as well. In the bathroom, washing his hands, he didn't need to open the medicine cabinet or towel closet. Everything was scrubbed clean.

He felt both pain and relief. He wanted to stride into the kitchen, take her in his arms, and say something just right, to ease her heart and deny his meanness. Why couldn't he love her? What was wrong with him? He went into the kitchen almost light-headed from tension. She was seated at the side of the table, which she always chose, being on his right instead of the opposite end.

"I think this house has become very heavy with lonesomeness," he said, and pulled out his chair.

She was silent, so he made himself look directly at her. She was all right. Her features were calm enough although there was a little high color across her cheeks.

"I'd rather you missed me than be wishing me gone."

The accuracy of it eased him. She was a smart woman.

"You deserve better than me."

"Agreed."

He was a bit alarmed.

"I didn't mean it," she said.

"We're outdoing each other."

She nodded.

She had moved everything personal back while he was gone. After supper, they packed up her dishes and took them to her house, and brought his back. They put off the other things for the next couple of days.

"I'm going to sleep at my place tonight," she said. "It'll be hard for me, hard for both of us, I hope, but it's better to be quick and strong."

He didn't argue. The more she talked, the more she was the winner here, and he could give her at least that much.

So when he watched the late-night news, he was alone again, aware of the quietness of his breathing, of the house itself. He was in the last part of his life. He just couldn't find a real niche. He watched the weather map and paid attention to what it was doing in Oklahoma, and in Idaho where the National Old Time Fiddlers contest was always held, and back east for Amy, and the whole state of Missouri, where Cora had returned. He didn't have his lady jammers. He didn't really have anything. He put on a tape, went to bed. He could barely hear the music. He pulled back the covers. Fresh sheets. Tears threatened. He swallowed and lay down.

He thought of Dolores in her hospital bed, a mind that didn't know anything but itself and couldn't count on that. Hurting. No understandable comfort.

He closed his eyes. He hoped he hadn't injured Callie's heart and believed he hadn't. His hurt, but he had it coming. None of them could be other than what they were.

Maybe that was true of Elizabeth too.

⌣

A week and a half later, when the hospital was releasing Dolores, Carl told Dave Stone he was taking the next two days off. "Maybe more days next week. I'll have to see how it goes and let you know."

"This is the busiest season," Stone said. "I don't think I can allow you to tell me when your vacation is."

222

"Do you want me to quit? You're always looking for a reason to tell me to get out. Maybe you'd like to shoo away the whole world. All right. You got it." Carl reset his hat and headed for the front door.

"No," Stone said from behind him. "I don't want you to quit."

The proper response, Carl knew, was to say, *Well too bad, I quit anyway.* He didn't do it. Instead, a little surprised at his own words, he said, "That's what I thought."

On the way to the hospital he stopped at a corner market and bought one of their cellophane-wrapped flowers. It was a little wilted, but a flower still. He bought candy too, but then he worried that Dolores's jaw might still be tender, so he gave the candy to the nurse he liked. "She's the nicest person when she's normal," the woman said. "It's a pity."

"She does rally," Carl said. "Got some fight in her."

He went into Dolores's room. She was looking out the window. She turned around. Framed in light from behind, with her hands clasped at her waist, she could have been a young girl, a bride, maybe, shy and hopeful.

"Now you're a pleasant sight," he said.

"So are you."

Carl chuckled. Combative little thing. He didn't know why she pleased him so, but she did. When they left, Carl guided and supported her in the old-fashioned way, by offering his right arm, then pressing his left hand over hers. It felt so right that he was momentarily frightened. He didn't want to get old now, didn't want to die now. Maybe something wonderful was just around the bend. He raised her hand to his lips briefly, then opened the car door. He'd never noticed that her fingers had dimples, soft indentations above each knuckle. "I've been thinking," he said, "that maybe you'd do better if you didn't feel so alone. You might just move in with me awhile." He shut the door, and, going around to his side, stopped for a moment to light a cigarette and compose himself. Strong emotions in a man weren't too becoming.

$$\backsim$$

Carl bought a run-down old house with rambling rooms and high ceilings and many doors, and hired a carpenter—who was also a fine fiddler—to pretty it up. Carl took charge of Dolores's medicine. He called her from the Emporium three times a day. She took over the cooking, but he helped her with the dishes and cleaning. "I didn't marry you for a slave," he said, though they hadn't married yet. It was his introduction of the possibility. She noted it, he saw, and didn't reject it.

He knew she would go crazy again, and again. She had a fire in her that would've burned up a fiddle if she'd been a musician. But she'd always come back to being a sweet, loving creature. She was both. And maybe he was supposed to help women. Looking back, that's what he'd done over and over, good or bad. This one, he knew, was worth it. Maybe they all were. No maybe to it.

$$\backsim$$

On a Saturday afternoon Carl came home, saw Dolores at the clothesline. He checked the mail on his desk and reheated the morning coffee. He took his cup and the *National Old Time Fiddlers Association Newsletter* into the living room. He settled back in the easy chair he used when no one was visiting. He unfolded the newsletter. He almost dropped the cup. His picture was on the front page, below a caption reading, "The Fiddlers' Fiddler: Tribute to Carl 'Pop' Bradshaw." He didn't recognize the photograph, but it was about how he looked now. He had on a dress bow tie and his best hat. They must've blown up a snapshot taken at some fiddle contest.

The head and neck of a guitar was barely visible behind him, and if he could place the guitar, he'd know when and where the picture was taken. But he couldn't. The instrument was too blurred. The backup could have been Amy. Cora. Could be so many people. He couldn't read the article right then. He had to stand up and look out the window awhile, have a cigarette, turning and looking at the newsletter every few moments like it was a woman he was too shy to approach. He felt absolutely skittish. He opened the front door and stood on the porch with his hands clasped behind him, rocking back on his heels. "I'll be damned," he said.

When the flush left him, he entered the house. He picked up the newsletter, read the first two paragraphs while standing, then sat down. Somebody had done a lot of digging. There was his whole history: his dad's and mom's birth states, their full names; the name of the farm they'd leased and the one his dad finally owned; where and when Carl'd won his first contest, with his mother playing rhythm. And the writer had quoted a bunch of people. Harold Rendon: "He'll teach a competitor his own hot licks, loan his fiddle to anyone who asks, give away his strings. He doesn't compete the way most people do. Carl has higher rules." Byron Milburn: "Carl Bradshaw treats musicians, audiences, and most of all, music, with respect. He always dresses up to play, even if he's jamming. 'You have to court a good melody,' he told me. 'Just coax it out of the strings. Treat it like something of value.'" Amy Vanderveen: "He tapes jams at his house, and when a musician visits at another time, he'll play the tape like it just happened to be in the machine, and there will be one of the best tunes that person ever played. Pop helps people sound good. His melody is underneath everyone's. He's the only fiddler I know who overpays his backups. Most guitarists would pay *him* to let them play along." Billy Wilcox: "I count knowing Carl Bradshaw as the best fortune of my life. Every hot lick in my repertoire he either taught me or got bored doing better than I do now. The man doesn't have a jealous, mean, or competitive streak in his entire body. He's not only the best fiddler I know, he's the best man. He still helps me. I beg a lesson from him at least once a year." On and on. Somebody had talked, too, about those silver dollars for young contestants. No name on that one, but he knew. Cora.

Carl thought the pleasure might stop his heart. He put the newsletter aside. If he read it again right now, he'd be glorifying himself. People's affections made liars out of them. He wasn't a fool. But he was grateful. He said that aloud to his empty house.

Dolores came in with a full basket. She glanced at the desk. "You look at your mail?" she asked.

"Some of it."

"Some of it is pretty nice."

"You read that, did you?"

"I'm going to make a bunch of copies and save them in plastic."

"Whatever you want," he said. "It doesn't matter to me." He immediately regretted the pretense. "It might be a nice thing to do."

He leaned his head back and watched sunlight and shadow play through the living room. He wasn't that good a man. Nobody was. Nobody was adequate to every person's needs. But this was a wonderful time of life. The afternoon glowed all around, soft, like spring would last forever, like bad things had been undone, made right, forgiven. Somewhere behind him, Dolores began humming. It was something she did often now. Sometimes he recognized the tune as one he fiddled, but she never got too loud. She had a real good ear and was right on key—he had a little bit of harmony living in the house with him. All in all, he was happy, and he wasn't sure if that just happened or if it had been there all along. It didn't matter. He wished the rest of the world such luck.

ACKNOWLEDGMENTS

I thank my writing friends whose time, expertise, honesty, and tenderness (yes) helped bring this work to completion: Chuck Hocter, Renee Nagel, Jim Taylor, and Chanda Zimmerman (Blackwater Literary Society); Debra Brenegan, Trudy Lewis, and Phong Nguyen (Mid-Mo Writers); my first partner in creative writing and at *Pleiades* (UCM), Kevin Prufer, who said all along *The Universe Playing Strings* was a good book; my friends everywhere who have both supported and forgiven my obsessions; my dear husband, Baird Allen Brock, for his calm faith through drafts and drafts; and my daughter, Kristine Lowe-Martin, for her unstinting patience, generosity, fondness, and sharp intellect.

My deepest gratitude to the University of New Mexico Press, especially to Elise McHugh. Without her insight and guidance I wouldn't have seen the real promise of the book.

And, of course, a loving bow to the boundless community of musicians.